Published by Ebtehal Mohmed

Copyright © 2021 Ebtehal Mohamed Elmeshay

All Rights Reserved

This book has mature content (18+)

Trigger warnings/ general warnings:

Physical and Verbal abuse, Talks of suicide, Smut, Death, Relationship with an Age Gap (19 and 23), Organised Crime/ Gangs, Happy relationships : (

This is a fast paced romance/ crime novel.

This book, and all characters, locations and businesses are a mere figment of my imagination, unless stated otherwise, and is not for education purposes.

Thank you.

Hey Abby…

…This one's for you, I love you ♡

Lots of love, eby

"You have a home in my heart."

- Elias Kader

Aloura West ♡

Chapter One

Aloura Olea West had only ever cried four times in her life. The first time was, naturally, when she was born. Her mother said she'd wailed for hours, joking that she must have been psychic; crying because she knew she was now stuck in this fucked up world.

If only she knew how true her words would turn out to be.

But naive Aloura used to laugh when she told her that story. She had found it amusing; how can a baby, who was mere seconds old, be able to see the future?

Her mother would laugh along and say, *"you're just special like that."* And ever since then, Aloura would sit at her mother's feet, hands on her mother's knees, chin resting on the backs of her hands, yearning to hear the same story again and again. How she'd cried for hours, and nothing seemed to stop her, and after that, she didn't cry for a long period of time.

Her mother said that was when she must have accepted her fate, and to that, Aloura would giggle, calling her mother "silly" for believing that.

The second time she cried was in kindergarten, when Jasmine had drawn all over her Mother's Day card when Aloura had gone to the bathroom. Mrs Anderson sat with her for hours, consoling her and offering to make a new one together.

But Aloura refused, instead, giving her mother the ruined card- pretending the scribbles were her idea. "What's that?" Her Mum pointed to the long messy lines over the glittery flower.

"That's fog" She grinned at her mum, she'd pushed her tears to the back of her eyes, heartbroken at the fact the mother had noticed the scribbles before the flower she'd spent ages cutting perfectly.

"Fog?" Mother laughed. "Why've your drawn fog?"

"To show you I'll always love you even I can't see you"

The third time She ever cried was at her mama's funeral. She couldn't even speak when she was asked to say her last words to her mother. She wanted to yell at everyone for saying that. They weren't her last words. Mother told her she'd always be there, if not my presence, by spirit.

And Aloura believed her.

Her mother had always told her that she would one day become the kisses in the wind, the melody that the trees danced to. She was the guiding hand that would constantly push her to be her best.

To be perfect.

She promised Aloura to always be with her; that she could talk to her anytime and she'd hear her. So Aloura stood at the podium, with shaking hands and tear stained cheeks. Sobbing.

They wouldn't understand she'd told herself, *they don't know what my mum said.*

Her father had pulled her down and into to his chest after a minuet of her standing there in silence, he held her tightly. And in that moment, as they cried together, he knew he had to be both the mother and father for his little girl.

Except he'd prove to be none.

And the fourth time was now. As she stood at the edge of the building.

Her pale bruised hands gripping the cold metal bars behind her. She wasn't suicidal or waiting for the perfect time to jump. In fact, the opposite.

She stood at the edge of dying in hopes of feeling alive for mere seconds. She had done this routinely after her mother had died and her father switched; becoming a person she no longer recognised. It was almost an escape, sitting at the rooftop.

"Are you going to jump?" A girl's voice called over her shoulder. She turned around, startled. She wasn't, but had she scared her the slightest bit more, she would have accidentally plummeted to her death.

Aloura ignored the intruder. Turning her head towards the city below her. It never failed to amaze her how small everything looked from up here. How insignificant everyone was. She wondered if this was God's view; and if this is what he saw, why had he zeroed out her mother to take away? "Suit yourself, psycho" the women called, "just tell your family not to sue the apartment complex."

What family Aloura wanted to call back at her, *my deadbeat father? Or dead mother?* But she bit her tongue. Mother always stressed to her about stranger danger.

The women looked around thirty years old, and had she not opened her mouth, Aloura would have said she looked welcoming. Aloura had turned to the stranger, studying her silently. The women had short black hair, with a few white strands spreading through. It was tied in a loose bun at the back of her head. She wore a blue tank top over her slightly chubby body, and some white pyjama bottoms. "They won't" Arielle finally spoke, "because I'm not going to jump"

The old women rolled her eyes and turned around away from Aloura, "stupid emotional teenagers" she muttered loud enough for Aloura to catch wind of her cold words. "They really think the world revolves around them." She walked to the blue door a few feet away, her sliders scraping the concrete beneath her harshly. The large door slammed behind her, and Aloura cringed, the sound of her stride had reminded her of her drunken father's feet grazing the kitchen floor every morning.

I'm not a teenager, Aloura wanted to call after her. Even though she was. Nineteen to be exact, but she acted a lot older. She felt like she'd lived a lot longer too- she was ready to give up on this thing called life. But she wasn't suicidal. She wasn't trying to die, but she wasn't trying to stay alive either. She liked to call it floating. But sometimes, a large wave takes over and rips the breath from her lungs. Suffocating her until her ears would ring from the sound of her echoing scream. Except no one else seemed to hear it, and everyone else around her seemed to be floating fine as she drowned. If her screams weren't defeating, she swore she would have been able to hear their laughter.

Aloura's phone rang, snapping her out of her haze. She let her trembling hands momentarily go from the railing behind her, using one hand to balance herself onto the ledge and the other to dig deep into her pocket. Kaden was calling her.
Aloura loved Kaden. Or at least she said she did. But she wasn't sure if it was her or anyone else she was trying to convince.

She had met him before her mother had died, and he was there for her during her hardest times. But he was currently in his second year of college, three hours away. He called regularly- regularly being used loosely- to bloat about his new friends and all the parties he'd attended. Aloura couldn't help but envy him. He got to go to college, he's living the dream; two parents in one home, while he's away in college, a girlfriend that he calls every now and then, and drugs and alcohol every night. Her finger lingered over the decline button before she sighed loudly and pressed accept.

"Hey babe!" His voice boomed through the phone. But instead of his girlfriend, the wind greeted him, Aloura didn't know what to say. The last time they'd spoken they'd argued. "What's that sound Aloura?" He called over the deafening music. If Aloura wasn't so upset she'd have found it ironic, amusing even. "You're not at that god awful roof top again, are you?"

Aloura sighed, choosing to ignore his last statement. She knew how much he hated this place, scared he'd one day be scraping her pieces off the pavement below. "What do you want Kaden?"

"Get off the edge and then we can talk" Aloura paused for a moment, she didn't want to talk, nor go on the other side. But for the sake of their relationship- or whatever was left of it- she complied. Placing the phone under her chin, she leaned back onto the metal bars, before swinging her legs back to safety. "This isn't because of what we last spoke about, right babe?" Kaden asked after he was certain his girlfriend now had both feet on solid ground. His voice sounded hopeful, and Aloura knew he wanted her to reassure him- even if it was with lies.

I wouldn't call it talking Aloura thought to herself, kicking a stray rock onto the wall. *More like me listening and you yelling. Even though I should have been the upset one.* Again, she held her tongue. "I wasn't going to jump Kaden" she groaned again, what was it with people thinking she was suicidal? It wasn't like she was crying whilst hanging off a building.

"Promise me you won't" he asked quietly.

Aloura rolled her eyes, she didn't believe in promises, it was a way people literally ask to be disappointed. "Promise I'm not going to jump" *Not over you and your stupid female friends anyway.* "Did you want anything?"

"Oh yeah" Kaden grinned on the other side of the phone, "I might come to Cambro soon." Aloura paused, not sure how she was going to fake excitement.

"Oh wow," she cringed at her effort, "That's great"

Kaden paused for a moment and let out an awkward laugh. "What's wrong? Are you not excited to see me?" he joked, but the words lingered between them, they both knew the answer.

"No god no" Aloura rushed out, "I am excited. I'm just busy with work and dad, you know?"

Kaden didn't know. He'd not seen her dad since her mother's funeral. Kaden and Aloura were childhood lovers, he'd even met her mother, and parts of Aloura knew that's why she'd kept him around. Her mother approved of him; how would she ever approve of another now she's dead?

After her mother's death, Kaden was no longer invited into her home, and even when he'd brought it up, Aloura would shut down the idea before the idea could fester. He'd not failed to notice how much Aloura had changed after losing her mother. How she'd skip school and could no longer hang out for long. In the rare occasions she did, he'd watched her run home- almost like she was fearful of what would happen if she wasted a single second. But he'd brushed it off as her grieving.

"How is the old man?" Kaden asked after a moment, Aloura's breath hitched in her throat, she didn't want to talk about her dad to Kaden, to anyone even.

"He's good"

"I've not seen him in a while" Kaden noted awkwardly.

"Neither have I Kaden, he's a surgeon." Aloura cringed at her white lie, hoping her mother was too busy with her angel duties to have heard her daughter spew out lies. Aloura however, found solace in the fact she wasn't completely lying. Her father really was a surgeon, an unemployed one, but still qualified.

"of course, of course-" Kaden laughed before being interrupted by a set of drunken giggles.

"Kay baby what are you doing out here? The party's inside." The girl slurred. Aloura in turn closed her eyes tightly, before walking to the edge of the roof top and looking up at the stars.

"Yeah Kay" she laughed but no humour evident in her voice, "don't keep your friend waiting."

"She really is just a friend baby I swear-" Kaden frantically spewed out before Aloura hung up; too tired to listen to the reoccurring words that seemed to show up in every conversation.

Aloura slid the phone into her back pocket and looked at the sky, spotting a blinking star amongst the freckles of light that littered the sky. Her mother had told her she would one day sit on the brightest star and watch down at her daughter.

"A blinking star means someone is smiling down at you" her mother had told her. Aloura watched the blinking star for a moment before smiled back and closed her eyes momentarily. She could have sworn she noticed her mother smile lighting up the sky when she'd reopened them.

"God" she whispered sadly, "I only miss you when I'm breathing Mama"

Chapter Two

Aloura found comfort in the rooftop. She had originally found this place when she had reached the lowest point in her life. She stood at the edge, counting down the seconds before midnight would strike and would officially mark her mother's second death anniversary. But she'd noticed how alive she felt as she struggled to balance onto the edge. How her mind begged her to go back onto safe grounds. The way her heart beat a little faster with every passing second. A ticking reminder that despite the numbness that seemed to submerge her, she was still alive.

Maybe I don't want to die, she'd thought to herself, loosening her grip on the handles behind her. Maybe I just want to feel alive.

She'd wondered if those before her had come to the same conclusion she had. If others religiously came to this rooftop to stand at the edge, scrambling for momentarily feelings of high. She wondered if others too were addicted, if they had one day decided this momentarily high wasn't enough. If they too now sat with her mother in the stars looking down at her. Watching her take the same path they did.

Aloura's mind had wondered to Kaden, she swallowed back the bile as she thought of the possibility of another's hands roaming his body. Aloura pushed through her tears, she didn't want her cry count to become five; she hated odd numbers.

Aloura smiled up at the sky, "how many times have you cried?" She asked the clouds. It thundered back in response, and Aloura giggled quietly. She had embarrassed the sky. In response, the clouds spat down fat droplets onto the ground, and Aloura grinned cheekily. Her eyes caught the blinking star in the distance, and she smiled softly. Her mother was telling her to get home before she got sick.

Aloura was too engrossed with the sky to have noticed the young man that stood below her. He had wanted to call out to the stranger and reassure them there were better options, but he knew his cries would fall upon deaf ears.

He wondered how insignificant he looked down here. Maybe this is why God hasn't been answering my prayers. He let out a breath he didn't know he was holding as Aloura answered her phone and swung her legs over the edge.

He wasn't sure why he cared if she'd jump or not, he hated people, and people hated him. Maybe his ears were so desperate to hear how things would all be okay, that if he said it aloud he'd be able to convince his eyes it wasn't his lips moving. But without speaking a word to the girl, he'd walked away, his mind replaying how peaceful she looked at the edge. Wishing to the stars he'd one day find his momentarily high.

♡ ♡ ♡

Aloura had gotten halfway home before she'd realised how much trouble she'd gotten herself into. It was way past midnight, and her father had expected her to cook his dinner. Part of her wanted to turn around and sleep under the slide in the playground like she had done plenty of times before. But she knew it was impossible when she had work tomorrow.

Aloura grew restless as the familiar building came to review. She wished she could have a resting place, where she sighed in relief when it came in view. But instead, the place she used to race her mother to, became the place she ran from. She found it ironic how she'd been running for so long but not strayed far.

Aloura's shaky hands pressed down onto the cold metal handle, twisting it and pushing the door ajar softly. Her breath held itself in her throat. She was too scared to breathe, this was no way of living. The door creaked softly as Aloura helplessly forced her body through the small gap. The hallway was dark, and no sign of her father greeted her. That is, if you don't consider the mountains of beer bottles that littered the floor a sign. Aloura pushed the door silently, kicking past the heap of unopened bills that lay scattered around the floor.

She made her way into the once comforting home, only to be greeted by her father's snoring figure, sprawled uncomfortably on the couch. The television blared out a random game show. If her situation wasn't so depressing, Aloura would laugh at how money hungry her father was, yet still refused to work.

Aloura walked into the living room, the smell of alcohol and cigarettes permeated through the room. She picked up the remote and switched it off before turning to her snoring father. She knew she had to help him to his room- she didn't want to face the consequences of leaving him on the couch again.

"Come on dad" she groaned hoisting him up. But to no avail, he remained seated, light snores escaping his lips. "Help me please" she groaned to him. Aloura's dad, Michael, was no longer the fitness and health obsessed father everyone seemed to remember him as. He now sported a stubbly beard, opposed to his usual clean-shaven face. His healthy body now larger, a beer belly hanging before him.

Michael groaned at the movement around him, his head was pounding and with every movement his daughter made, his anger seemed to grow. "Where the fuck were you?" he slurred, his eyes half open.

Aloura's body froze at the sound of his voice, "work" she lied through her teeth. "But come on dad, you have to help me get you to bed." Aloura attempted to change the subject, fearful her father would start talking with his hands.

"don't call me dad" he snapped, his hand lazily finding Aloura's curls and tugging at them harshly. "Understand?" he forced her head to look down at him. Aloura nodded fearfully, and with another tug at her hair she realised her mistake.

Rule number four: verbal responses. "Yes sir" she muttered. Rule number two: call me sir.

Aloura was never sure why her father had given her such extensive and extreme rules. She'd always believed the sir one was merely a way he detached himself from her, and in turn her mother. I guess he feels less guilty when the girl he's laying his hands on refers to him as sir rather than dad.

"Good bitch" he spat out, his hand connecting with her cheek. His head was now moving in an ungainly manner as Aloura supported his weight. They moved painfully slow across the hall and up the stairs. When they'd reached his room, Aloura used her body to push the door open, before helping his now sleeping body onto the bed. She had originally made no attempt to make him comfortable or cover him, but as she turned to leave, she found herself turning back to him. Hesitantly moving the covers up, before digging through his drawers and placing Advil at the nightstand.

Goodnight, dad. She thought to herself as she stepped out the door. Too fearful to say the words out loud. She wasn't sure if it was his hands on her body that hurt more when she referred to him as dad, or the rejection and disgust that filled his eyes.

Aloura made her way to her room- or if she could call it that. It remained plain and undecorated as before her mother died. They were going to do it together, and it felt too painful to do it without her. Not that she could anyway, Aloura was the sole provider, and with the stacking bills, and her dad's addiction to both alcohol and fags, she barely had any money left for food, let alone decorating.

Parts of Aloura never attempted to decorate in hopes of moving to college, decorating her room would mean she had accepted this prison as her home, and Aloura would draw her last breath before that happened.

Everything was going well, Aloura had saved enough money to help start a life away from her father, but after getting wind of his daughters plans, Michael was quick to spend her hard-earned cash on alcohol and gambling. And Aloura could do nothing to turn back the time and take back her father's detrimental actions.

Aloura laid on her bed, her mind was racing. She hated thinking, she hated being left alone with her mind. It dragged her to dark places she hoped to never revisit again. But with the silence bouncing off the walls, Aloura felt herself submerged yet again, alone, with her dark thoughts.

Chapter Three

The sun seeped through the broken blinds, startling Aloura. She shot out of bed and scanned her surroundings, when she was certain her father wasn't in the room with her, she relaxed back onto the bed, sighing in relief. Her mornings always consisted of a startled wake, followed by a few seconds of paralysing fear, before she'd scan the room for her father. Out of the many years spent living like this, Aloura had only located her father in her room twice.

The first time, he was innocently checking on his daughter. The guilt of the beating he'd given her the night before had left him pacing the entire morning. He'd entered her room in hopes of apologising, but one sight of his sleeping daughter and he lost track of time. Images of her at peace still linger in his mind, and the panic he witnessed his daughter go through as she spotted him by the doorway made his heart break a little more. So, when she left that day for school, he promised to change his ways. He'd cleaned the house, and even poured down the remaining alcohol down the sink- something he came to regret barely hours later. As the images of his dead wife, and flinching daughter made his hands itch for a drink. A means to forget, and so he gave in.

The second time, he had started drinking before lunch- which was unusual. His anger seemed to strengthen as he realised he was grieving in the living room alone, whilst his daughter slept the day away. He'd marched to her room, and flung the door open before making his way over her. Aloura didn't have to search the room for her father's presence that day, his hands were enough of an indicator.

"You don't love her" he growled, throwing the covers off the shivering, sick girl.

Aloura sat up gasping, her hands clutching her head. She flinched back into the corner of the bed as soon as she noticed her father's presence. Her bolting up awake had caused her head to spin, and the lack of Aloura's denial of his accusation burned Michael within. "I fucking knew it." He snarled, grabbing her harshly by the arm. "You never fucking loved her."

"Loved who dad" Aloura cried, placing her small hands over her fathers in hopes of loosening his painful grip.

"You forgot about her already" he spat, pushing Aloura forcefully away from him. "She would be ashamed to call you her daughter."

After that day, Aloura's body seemed to have timed itself, waking her up every night after a couple of hours. Forcing her to look around her fearfully for her father's presence.

After Aloura had slipped on her work uniform, she made her way down the staircase. She placed her earphones in the hem of her trousers, too scared to have them in sight of her dad. He would definitely rip them apart, and Aloura could never afford to replace them immediately. She made her way into the kitchen for a glass of water. Although her last meal was lunch from the previous day, Aloura found herself rather starving than her father hungry. She didn't know whether it was because she still loved him or feared him. The beatings would definitely be worse if he's already in a bad mood from hunger.

Aloura didn't expect to find her father already awake, situated on the kitchen table, his head resting between his hands. Droplets of tears falling from his eyes and onto the newly cleaned countertop. Aloura halted her steps at the door, allowing her eyes to soak up the view before her. Her father had always gone through bi-polar moods of swearing to change, but Aloura had not seen him cry over something that was not her mother.

"Sir?" she asked softly making her way towards him. She cringed at the name, out of all the rules, she hated that one the most. "Are you-" she hesitated a little before swallowing her fear, "are you okay?"

Michael's head snapped up; he hadn't heard her daughter walk in. He quickly stood up and pushed the chair behind him. At the loud sudden noise and her father's abrupt movement, Aloura let out a shriek and stepped back. The chair fell back and as it echo of its impact on the floor died down, silence welcomed them. Aloura stared at her father's feet, calculating his movements, just in case.

"Aloura, honey" her dad's voice came out hoarse, "I'm so sorry"

Aloura could have sworn she'd heard those words before, but she dared not to say that aloud. Because at least he's apologising right? Some dads don't apologise.

Some dads don't beat their kids either. A voice in her muttered. Parts of Aloura were sick of this life. Parts of her wished it was her father that had died that night. But she immediately felt guilty after thinking that, yet she couldn't seem to shake off the thoughts of the life she'd have had. Maybe she'd be in college now, and her mother would have remarried and travelled the world like she always dreamed she would have.

"it's okay" Aloura breathed out a laugh, moving past her father to grab a glass and fill it with water. At her father's sceptical face, Aloura sighed, "really sir. Look" she moved her face around to show her face to him, "no bruises this time."

Michael visibly cringed at her use of 'this time' but he decided to find solace in the fact he hadn't hit her that bad, this time. "please" he paused, "call me dad."

"Okay dad" Aloura chirped before raising her glass to her mouth, a ghost of a smile lingering on her lips. "I should go dad," she rinsed the glass before putting it back in the cupboard, "bye dad." Dad, dad, dad. Aloura wanted to yell it aloud until her ears become familiar with the way it sounded from her lips. He'd told her to call him dad, a simple word she'd craved to call him ever since he'd first lay his hands on her.

Aloura practically skipped to work, the bounce in her feet and the smile plastered on her face were visible to everyone who took a moment to look. She pushed the front door to the bakery open, beaming at the head that turned to her as the bell sounded through the room. She walked up to behind the bar and into the staff only doors. "Agnes!" she called out happily as soon as she noticed the older woman's figure facing away from her. The blonde lady turned startled, before a matching smile broke into her face.

"Oh Bella!" she grinned as the younger girl made her way to her. Letting out a grunt as their body's collided, "careful dear, I'm getting old."

Aloura shushed her before apologising sheepishly, she was getting old, but one could barely tell. "Sorry Annie. I just didn't think you'd be back so soon."

"Yes, neither did I" Agnus laughed at the nickname her Bella had given as a toddler. Bella was, once, Aloura's nanny. At first, the little girl didn't like the idea of being left at home with a stranger while both her successful doctor parents went to work. But she was quick to realise how much fun Agnus had bought to her days. They'd bake, sing together and she somehow even made tasks such as cleaning and schoolwork fun. From the day Agnus had met Aloura, she'd called her Bella. Aloura despised the nickname.

"That. Is. Not. My. Name." The young girl would stomp. "If you call me that one more time, I'll- I'll" the girl stuttered, her mind unable to contrive a similar nickname in time. "I'll call you something worse."

'Like what?" Agnus smiled dearly.

"Like. Like Annie."

Except, ever since Agnus' teenage daughter's death, she'd longed to hear that nickname again. Agnus' daughter was a teenage mother, but the heartbreak of losing her child's father to another female had driven her into depression. And ultimately, suicide. She was left alone, with her grandchild, until Bella. So, Agnus smiled, and since that day, her heart had been filled.

"You don't work today. What're you doing here?" Aloura spoke as she attempted to tie her apron around her body.

"You didn't hear?" Agnus laughed at the girls attempts of tying her apron, she motioned for Aloura to turn around, "Joe's leaving."

"Really? Why?" Aloura gasped. She was happy he was leaving, she almost hated him. Aloura could have sworn he got paid to do nothing but complain. 'We should show him his job description, maybe he thought bitching was his job.' Cassidy would joke.

And when they had the night shift together, he'd slack off his work and leave most of the work for the staff during the morning shift. But when they had the morning shift, all he'd do is complain how the night staff were useless.

Agnus paused after tying a small bow at the girls back, hesitating before she spoke. "He's going to college."

Everyone at work knew Aloura's dreams of one day going to college, of becoming a doctor like her mother. But she'd been working for almost four years, with no end near.

"That's great!" Aloura pushed a smile on her face before grabbing a tray of baked goods and heading to the front desk to refill them. Aloura's mind spun as she worked, images of others living their dreams while she was stuck in this bakery filled her mind. Aloura pushed through the negative thoughts.

He told me to call him dad, she grinned, *do you think he'll let me say I love you next? Or tell me about Mama.*

Baby steps, she told herself, maybe we can really be a family again.

Aloura was too busy grinning at the life her and her father could live, that she missed the sound of the bell signalling a customer had walked in. It was only until he had waited at the till, watching the grinning girl, did he scoff out loud, snapping her attention to him.

"I'm so sorry" she laughed awkwardly, "I'll be with you in one moment" she turned to place the large tray onto the counter before grabbing a towel to wipe down her hands. "How can I help you today?"

"By serving me on fucking time" he grumbled under his breath, and Aloura fought the urge of throwing the towel in the guy's face.

"Yeah, I apologise about that," she smiled, knowing her job wasn't worth losing for a one-time customer. He scoffed in response. He didn't actually care he was served moments later than he'd liked, he just hated seeing others smile. If he was miserable, everyone else had to be.

"Yeah whatever" he rolled his eyes, his annoyance growing at the smile that seemed to never leave the workers lips.
He looked at the food displayed before him, before his eyes caught sight of the 'hiring' sign on the glass. "You're hiring?"

"Depends on who's asking" she forced out. Praying he wasn't thinking of working there, she had just gotten ridden of Joe, she didn't need an even ruder college.

"Me" he raised an eyebrow.

"Then no." she smiled sweetly, "anything else I can help you with?"

"For someone who was about to commit suicide last night, you sure are a bitch." He growled, Aloura flinched a little, taken aback by his words.

"What?" she whispered; her eyes wide.

"I said, for who was about to commit suicide last night, you sure are a bitch"

"I heard what you said" her eyebrows furrowed, her voice came out strained and the *guy* almost felt bad for his words. "I wasn't trying to kill myself" she muttered, slightly annoyed by the number of times she's had to reassure strangers she wasn't going to jump.

"Yeah, because you were hanging off the edge of a rooftop for fun, right?" he scoffed. He wasn't sure why he was telling her that he'd saw her, but the anger he'd bottled up all week seemed to be exploding on a random stranger.

"Bella?" Agnus' voice called from behind her, "what are you guys talking so angrily about?"

"Nothing." Aloura frowned; the happy mood she'd worked so hard to get suddenly souring.

Agnus frowned at the disorientated looking girl, before turning her attention to the man that looked at her with almost guilty eyes, "and who might you be?" she broke the silence grinning at him.

"I'm Elias."

Chapter Four

Much to Aloura's dismay, Annie had invited him to a drink on the house, to which he declined, but his denies were ignored as Annie turned to Aloura and asked her to fetch a menu.

"Order whatever you like honey. It's on the house" Agnus smiled at Elias, "Aloura" she turned to the scowling girl and nodded in his direction. Aloura knew what Agnus was doing, she had always pestered her about getting a 'husband'.

"Annie, I'm with Kaden." Aloura would remind the woman every time she tried to match her with a customer.

"Don't let you boyfriend stop you from finding you soulmate" she'd laugh, apparently, a phrase her granddaughter lived by. Aloura scowled as Agnus pinched the girl discreetly, a silent threat to get the girl to act properly. Aloura sighed and moved past Agnus, grabbing a menu and placing it in front of Elias.

"What can I get you today?" she asked him after a moment of his eyes scanning the menu. Agnus smiled and moved to the back of the store, leaving the two unattended.

"I'll have a black coffee and avocado and chicken bagel" Aloura noted his order, before asking if he'd like anything else, "that'll be all Bella"

Aloura raised an eyebrow at the nickname, as she went to retreat the menu, but made no effort to correct him. "Alright, it'll be out in a moment." She placed the menu where she'd retrieved it and walked towards the tray of baked goodies she'd discarded when Elias had rudely interrupted her. They settled in the silence, but she didn't miss how he'd watched her the entire time and scowled at her whenever their gazes met.

They remained in silence until Elias had finished his meal, Agnus stalked over to them. "Did you eat honey?" she'd asked him, and he smiled softly, mumbling an embarrassed thank you. "oh, Aloura why don't you pack some of those pastries for him to take?"

Both Aloura and Elias went to protest, but Agnus shushed them, and stalked over to Aloura to complete the task herself. She reached for the largest takeaway box and began selecting the fresh pastries. She had overpacked the box to the point it wouldn't close. Aloura rolled her eyes and went to help. after they'd boxed it, they handed it to a thankful Elias, "oh right, Annie? Right?" to which Aloura scowled at him.

"its Agnus to you." Aloura snapped, as Agnus offered him an apologetic look.

'Right. Agnus, sorry" his hand reached to rub the back of his neck awkwardly, "you're hiring?"

Agnus beamed and reached for an information leaflet before finding there wasn't any. "Oh, sorry Hon. We're out" she stood straight, "but pop back in tomorrow and I'll give you one."

Elias nodded, lifting the box of pastries and mumbling, 'thanks for this' and with one last look at Aloura, he walked out the bakery. Agnus and Aloura's eyes remained trained on the door until his figure disappeared.

"Oh! The chemistry." Agnus laughed, clasping her hands excitedly. Aloura's gaze left Elias' retreating figure and focused on the beaming manager before chucking a towel at her.

Aloura had finished work a couple of hours later and had made her way into the vacant home. Her father was nowhere in sight, and Aloura wasn't sure if she should have been relieved or not. Was he out drinking? Or looking for a job, considering he had vowed to change his alcoholic ways.

Aloura decided to hope for the latter but prepare for the former, she had started cleaning out the kitchen and moved to the living room when she'd noticed a broken photo frame on the floor. With hesitant shaking hands, she reached down and picked it up. It was a photo of her, her mother and father. She was on her father's shoulders, one of his large hands was gripping her ankle, and his other holding her mother's smaller hands. Even while alive, her mother looked angelic. Her long blonde locks fell down her shoulders and a yellow dress hung off her loosely, dancing with the wind.

Aloura couldn't help but notice how little space her mother took up, and despite the smile that was plastered on her lips, a broken home was reflecting in her eyes. Aloura ran her thumb against her mother's face, a large crack covering her, "What were you hiding mama?"

After a few moments, Aloura placed the photo frame up right on the shelf, before walking towards the basement, hopeful she'd find a photo frame in there.

There was nothing interesting in the basement, her father had moved a lot of her mother's belongings down there after seeing them became unbearable. Aloura had always found it weird how quick he was to dismiss her mother's actual death yet mourn so much. But she never had the courage to question him, her father didn't know how to talk without his fists.

Aloura walked towards a box of her mother's pictures, searching for the right sized frame. But her eyes caught a box pushed to the back. It was taped shut. Aloura pulled it from its placed and frowned at how securely shut it was- her father was always drunk and had not bothered to care for any other belongings he'd placed here. So why this box? Maybe that was what pushed Aloura to open it, but ten minutes later and Aloura was flicking through a selection of journals and letters in her mother's handwriting.

Michael knows I know. The top of one sheet read, Aloura furrowed her eyebrows. Was her father up to something? When did her mother find out? Was it what got her killed? Aloura wasn't actually sure if her mother was killed, but her father had always acted weird and hid her death certificate- so Aloura could only speculate.

Aloura can never know, we agreed. I won't tell the police, and Aloura is safe. I'm sorry.

Safe from what? She thought. Sorry for what?

Aloura shuffled through a few more pages, before she found a list of names, behind it a larger piece of paper was stapled to it. *Police. One side is with them.* Written hastily on the back. Aloura frowned again, she hated riddles and mysteries. "who's them mum?"

Aloura picked up another file of papers, *delivering you to evil*, written on the on the margins of the paper. Before Aloura could investigate for any longer, her father's car pulled into the driveway. Aloura shot up and scrambled to collect the papers from the floor, before stuffing them into the box. She picked up the list of names and placed it in her back pocket. 'I'll need this for later,' she thought.

'Aloura!" her father's drunken voice slurred through the hallways. Her heart stopped; she had figured he was sober if he was driving. She quickly grabbed an empty photo frame and shot out the basement. Her heart had begun beating so fast she could practically feel the pulsing in her tongue.

"Yes dad?" she asked him, parts of her still hoped that he still meant what he had said in the morning.

"Its sir you little bitch" he seethed, grabbing a handful of her hair. 'Now come here and tell me what's wrong with this view." He kept his filthy hands laced into Aloura's brunette locks as he dragged her into the kitchen. Her screams of pain did nothing to his stone cold heart.

Aloura's tear filled eyes scanned the room, fearful, before they landed on the empty kitchen table. Shit. *Rule number five; dinner is to be ready by five.* "Are you going to fucking tell me why my dinner isn't ready at my table?" Michael seethed, tugging at her hair with each word.

"Please, da-sir!" she cried, wrapping her hands around his wrists in an attempt to free herself from his painful grip. "I just thought" she stuttered before starting again, "this morning you said" "what did I say" he yelled; he grew impatient as she stumbled over her words.

"That you'll change and you're sorry" Aloura cried as he tugged once again at her hair, "so I thought we could do it together and bond." Although she had genuinely thought that earlier, she realised how stupid she sounded when she said them out loud. Her father was never going to change, and they'd never bond over anything. Unless she became alcoholic of course.

Michael scoffed and pulled one last time at her hair, forcing her to look up at him. Their eyes met and without warning, Michael's hand met Aloura's cheek. He let her hair go and she fell limp on the floor. She held her cheek in her hand and looked up at her father who looked down at her with disgusted eyes. "Get up you're dirtying my floor." He spat, grabbing a beer from the fridge. "Make one plate." He ordered, disgust evident in both his voice and his eyes. "Whores don't get to eat."

Aloura nodded and watched her father's retreating figure as it walked out the kitchen. "It's her death anniversary tomorrow." He spoke sadly when he reached the door, "don't fucking come home. I don't want to see you all day. Am I clear?" But Aloura already knew this- it had almost become a tradition in their household. Aloura swallowed and nodded.

"Crystal."

Chapter Five

Elias unbuttoned his collar shirt and threw his body onto the coach, his legs spread apart, taking the majority of the space in front of him. His apartment was small, it was all he could afford. But it was something, so he wasn't complaining. He sighed loudly and used his hands to rub his eyes roughly. He was tired, and angry.

Whenever life got one step better for him, it seemed to go two steps bad again, and he had no one but himself to rely on. He had become an orphan at the age of nineteen, with a ten-year-old brother who depended on him, which had forced him to grow up rather quickly. More so considering the shady stuff his father was involved it. Ones which he had to unfortunately take after him. Elias scoffed at the irony, other parents left their children homes and an inheritance, he got a debt with some dangerous people.

Things however, had reached a different level of dangerous after Elias had turned twenty-one, and concerned for his brother's safety, Elias had him removed from his care.

With thoughts of his brother permeating his mind, Elias sighed and reached at the coffee table in front him and grabbed his phone. He scrolled down the three contacts he had and pressed onto his brother's name.

It rang for a couple of minutes, before his now fourteen-year-old brother picked up the call. "Elias?" he sounded hopeful, and Elias closed his eyes painfully, he knew what his brother was going to ask, *again*. He had been having the same conversation for years now.

When the teenager received no reply, he repeated, this time concerned, which seemed to snap Elias from his daze. "Yeah, hi buddy." Elias sat up in his seat and leaned forward. "How are you?"

"Great" his brother chirped, "especially after I saw your gift. Thank you so much!"
Elias smiled softly from his end of the phone; his younger brothers happy voice was enough conformation he needed to know whether he'd made the right choice. "It was expensive. Right?'

"Don't worry about money Kalian" Elias sighed. He knew how much his brother was missing out with their lack of money, especially considering he would now miss out on friendships too if he didn't have the same gadgets to play together.

"You have enough though right?" Kalian's concerned voice tried again, "I know your trying to pay dads debts back. So, getting me a play station must have tightened things up right?"

Elias looked around his rundown apartment, he had turned the lighting and heating off to save money, and the only meal he'd had all week was the one Agnus had offered him earlier. "Not at all" he lied, "in fact, I went out to eat earlier and I bought a shit ton of pastries home to eat while I watch tv"

Elias didn't have a tv, but Kalian didn't need to know that. His lies seemed to settle the inner turmoil Kalian had, because he had soon forgotten about how expensive the gift was and began to ramble on why Elias should get one too so they can game together.

"We'll see buddy" Elias laughed, dismissing the young boys' words. There was no way Elias would splash the little money he had on useless things. Especially if they were for himself. "How's school?"

"Boring. I don't want to talk about school." Kalian groaned; he hated the education part of life. He had always blabbed about how he was going to drop out the second he had the option. But Elias knew he would never let that happen.

"That's good." Silence settled over them, and Elias closed his eyes in preparation for the question that was dying to be spilt from the start, "so" Kalian started, the clicking of his play station echoing through the call, "when can I move back with you?"

"I don't know bud. I'm trying, okay?" Elias used his thumb and index finger to rub his eyes harshly. Kalian didn't reply, so Elias continued, "I have work to do so, I'll catch you at another time?"

"Sure, bye Elias" Kalian mumbled sadly, before ending the call.

Kalian didn't mean to sound spoilt, but he missed the only family member he had. Living with family friends in Italy wasn't how he'd envisioned his life to be. Especially since when his older brother shipped him off two years ago, he promised it would be temporary. And two years and counting didn't feel like temporary at all.

"Are we going on holiday?" Kalian questioned, his short legs running to catch up with his older brothers' angry strides.

Elias ignored the younger boy, dragging the suitcase through the airport. After a moment he sighed, "I'm sending you to some trusted friends I know. But don't worry buddy, you'll be back before you know it."

The phone call soon ended, and as soon as Elias was certain his brother could no longer hear him, he shot up from his place on the couch. 'FUCK" he yelled out at no one in particular, before punching a whole through the wall. He stepped back, his nose flaring as he assessed the damage his fist had made. He groaned and clutched his hair at the sight of the broken wall, his landlord was going to have a field day with him. He had already warned him that his last hole in the wall was the last one he'd tolerate. Anymore and he would either be evicted or forced to pay the damages.

His apartment was small, with one bedroom, a living room, kitchen and a bathroom. It wasn't dirty by any means, Elias invested time and money to make it as homely as possible, with photos of their family around the apartment. But it was plain and boring. His kitchen was almost always empty, as the flat cost him almost all his monthly income. Making it extremely difficult to catch up with his dad's debt payments.

His dad was a good man- depending on who you asked. To Elias, he wasn't. his dad was hot headed and stubborn, and whatever he said, was what went. No room for objections or even suggestions were present when he'd decided on something. Which Elias guessed was what got them in this mess to begin with.

His mother had gotten cancer when he'd turned seventeen, and at first, they were all hopeful she'd recover. But as time went on, and she was beginning to struggle with simple tasks such as feeding herself. It was then that they'd all grown to know their days with her were numbered. His father didn't accept this. He couldn't stand the thought of losing his wife, so he searched for any possible means to help her.

He was approached by a doctor in the hospital about a trial for cancer patients. Its success rate was the best anyone had ever seen, but costly. Still, that wasn't enough to deter Elias' desperate father. He was re directed to a company, a shady one unbeknownst to him, and an agreement was made.

The trial was a hoax, a scheme to get the family to become in debt to powerful people, and thus, their puppets.

Elias' mother passed away when he'd turned nineteen, and his dad took his life a couple of months later, leaving the unpaid debts to his teenage sons.

Elias was snapped out his daze as his phone rang. He sent one last regretful look to the wall before walking towards his discarded phone.

Two missed calls from Blayde.

Elias pressed the notification, and held the phone to his ear, "hey man, what's up?" he called out when Blayde picked up.

"Don't what's up me dickhead, I've been ringing you, where you at?"

"You rang twice man." Elias laughed as he walked towards his bedroom to change out his suit. He didn't normally wear suits, but he had a job interview, and had hoped to make a good impression. "But what's up?"

"I'm just checking up. Don't forget the fight tonight. Boss might be there."

"Fuck."

"Fuck is right, pretty boy. So, you got to win this one. It's not just you arse on the line, its mine too."

"Yeah man, don't worry." Elias sighed as he opened his wardrobe, before bidding his mate farewell.

He threw his phone onto his bed and took out a comfortable change of clothes, before walking to the kitchen in hopes of finding a bite to eat.

The cupboards and fridge were practically empty, so he sighed sadly and made his way to his couch before his eyes caught the pastry box. He knew he shouldn't eat sweet things before a big fight, but it was that or fighting on a practically empty stomach. So, Elias grabbed the box and sat down. Internally thanking Agnus, and the spoilt child she worked with.

Chapter Six

A couple of hours later, Elias found himself in the changing rooms of an underground fighting arena. He was coming down from his sugar rush, and suddenly regretful for his decision of eating the sweet treats- regardless of how good they tasted.

"Keep your head in the fight bro" Blayde warned Elias in the locker rooms, "the boss is here tonight." he reminded him, but Elias already knew that. It was all he could think about all night.

Elias nodded and listened intently. He needed the money this month, it was the start of winter, and he was in desperate need for both heating and hot meals. Elias jumped in his place, an attempt at calming the jittering nerves that clawed through his body. "Don't worry man, I got this."

Blayde watched him with cautious eyes before hesitantly nodding. It wasn't that he didn't have faith in Elias, he was one of the best, but he tended to let his mind run in the ring. It only distracted him and gave his opponent leverage against him. "Come on, they're going to call your name any minute now."

Elias grabbed the water bottle, and squirted it into his mouth, before throwing it back into his bag. He grabbed his gloves and placed one on. Blayde grabbed the other and helped him into it before tapping his back in encouragement.

The pair walked out the locker and into the waiting area, they had barely halted their walk when Elias' name was called out. Elias looked at Blayde who nodded, silently reassuring him. He grabbed the mouth guard case and Elias opened his mouth. He clipped it in, before pushing Elias slightly to the door, following suit.

Elias was anxious, but he didn't show it. These sick people could read emotions even he didn't know he had, and the last thing he wanted was them using it to their advantage. The referee held up the ropes and Elias ducked his head and stepped into the ring. His opponent was already there. The crowd was going crazy, but Elias paid no mind to them, he wasn't here to be liked. He was here to win, get the money and one day find a way out.

The referee stepped into the middle and motioned for the boxers to walk closer. "Let have a clean fight, ya ear me?" he told them, his accent thick. Elias and his opponent nodded and looked at each other, both determined to be the victor tonight. "Good. Touch hands" the pair raised their gloves and tapped each other's.

"Okay. Back to your corners." He instructed. The pair followed his orders.

Elias watched his opponent jump around. He looked cocky, and his physique was much bigger than Elias' but that didn't deter him. *I need heating.* He reminded himself. *I need food.* He nodded his head at his own words. *I need Kalian back.* Elias could practically feel how full his stomach was going to be, and how warm his apartment was. He wiped his chin onto his shoulder and held his fists to his face, and the countdown began.

♡ ♡ ♡

"Fuck. Fuck. Fuck" Elias yelled out punching the locker with every curse word that spilled from his lips.

"Elias man, relax." Blayde sighed, they were both utterly and completely fucked, but they were in this mess together. Blayde never held it against Elias when he lost them a fight, he knew how hard it was. Especially having been in Elias' place before.

"How can I relax bro" he yelled; he was angry. "How can I relax" he repeated. "I just got my fucking ass handed to me out there. In front of the boss!" Elias walked away from Blayde and paced back and forth.

"We're fucked man. Rents due, I can't afford fucking food, Kalian keeps asking when he can come home. How the fuck do I tell him I'll forever be paying those bitches back?" he carried on.

"I know man, I know."

Blayde was in the same boat as Elias. Kind of at least. During a hard time in his life, he'd taken a loan. He was originally made a fighter, like Elias, but after a severe injury in the ring, the boss decided to use him as a trainer instead. Any money was better than no money to those people. And that's all they saw people like Elias and Blayde as. Money Makers.

"What the fuck was that princess play out there boys?" a taunting voice called out. The men froze at the masked man's voice and remained silent. He frowned at this. "I fucking asked you a question, so you answer it." The authority in his voice left no room for objection so Blayde spoke up.

"Sir. It's been getting hard, fighting with no food isn't-"

"I don't fucking care Blayde." The masked man growled, nodding his head towards one of his men to grab him by the collar. He was angry- the pair had just lost him a couple thousand. "Train your bitch better or-"

"The fuck did you call me" Elias moved to the boss threateningly, and the suited man dropped Blayde and turned to their boss, watching Elias' movements with weary eyes. Blayde was quick to react, grabbing his friend by the shoulder attempting to hold him back.

"Elias. Right?" the big boss grinned at Elias tauntingly, but he knew his name. "How is Kalian enjoying Italy?"

"Mother fucker." Elias stepped forward again only to be held back by a fearful Blayde who muttered a 'relax man' into his ear. Elias shrugged him off, although he knew his friend was right.

"Ah ah" the boss grinned, taking his own threatening steps towards the angry boxer. "Know your fucking place or your little brother will get it." Elias breathed through his nose angrily in response, "what? You don't like that?" he taunted. "How about that pretty lady you were with this morning?"

"Stay the fuck away from her." Elias found himself yelling. He wasn't sure why, he hated her, after all she was a spoilt little brat. He needed a job, and all she wanted to do was act pretentious. Elias didn't comment on it, but he had also seen the disapproved glance she had given Agnus when she'd offered him a meal. It wasn't like it was coming from her pay cheque.

"Then don't fucking lose again. "

And with that, he left, his two men following tow with a slam of the door. When the locker room door bang rang out, Blayde turned to Elias, a small smile playing on his lips. "There's a girl?" he grinned. "Is that why you weren't replying earlier?"

"Suck a dick man" Elias pushed Blayde out the way, a ghost of a smile lingered on his lips as Blayde's laughter filled the locker room.

The good mood, however, left Elias as fast as it came. The big boss' threat towards Kalian and Bella remained at the front of the boxer's mind "What do I do Blayde?" Elias' voice came out broken as he took a seat on one of the benches. He ran a hand through his hair in frustration. If Elias was alone, he was almost sure he would've let his tears fall.

Blayde paused for a moment, unsure on how to answer the visibly upset man. "What do you mean?" he asked, although he knew.

"This mess." Elias specified, "This life. I want to go to college, get a proper job and live with Kalian."

"I know bud." Blayde comforted him sadly, taking a seat beside him. They sat in silence, before Elias sat up and coughed awkwardly. The two friends had known each other for a while, but they'd never really spoke about their emotions.

"Anyway." He grabbed his bag, "I should go." Blayde nodded. And without another word, Elias walked out the changing room. Racking his brain for a spot he could smoke and take his mind off things.

The rooftop.

Chapter Seven

Aloura placed her father's hot dinner on the table, before walking towards the fridge and grabbing a cold beer. She placed it beside his cutlery and walked towards the living room.

Her father was as usual, sprawled on the coach engrossed in a loud game show displayed on the screen. He looked angry, he sounded angry too; yelling a string of curse words out at the competitor who'd lost out on some money. Aloura hesitated to call him, fearful his anger would become redirected at her, but if he didn't make it to his plate of food soon, it would go cold, which was a definite reason for him to beat her.

Aloura sighed sadly, knowing there was no good option. "Sir?" she asked, her voice barely above a whisper, and when he didn't reply, she moved father into the room, raising her voice slightly. His head snapped to her fearful figure angrily, if he wasn't so worked up about the money the man had just lost, he would have smirked at how much he scared her. "Your food" she continued, pointing to the kitchen.

Michael scowled but nodded, shooing the girl from his sight.

Aloura didn't have to be told to leave twice, she bolted out the room as fast as she could and ran towards her room. She picked up her first aid kit, and a large jumper and her phone before walking down the stairs and out the house.

It was her mother's death anniversary soon, and per tradition, Michael would force her out the house. He didn't want to see parts of the women he loved in his daughter. It was too much of a painful reminder. But that didn't bother Aloura, she enjoyed sitting on the rooftop and talking to her mother anyway.

Aloura made the trek journey towards the rooftop, her earphones blasting out music in an attempt to block out her own thoughts. When she'd arrived at the large apartment complex, she wasn't expecting to see Elias stood at the rooftop. It wasn't her's by any means, but it angered her that someone who spoke so cruelly to her had set foot on something so personal. She frowned at the sight of him leaning over *her* barrels. She scoffed and angrily made her way to the side of the building, marching up the stairs.

"What the fuck are you doing on my rooftop?" she called out as she entered the rooftop.

Elias turned around startled, he was already in a bad mood, and the whining brat was making his anger almost unbearable. He eyed her for a second, before placing his cigarette in between his lips, "Does your mummy and daddy own this apartment complex little girl?" he taunted. When he received no reply, he scoffed, "that's what I thought."

Aloura was taken back by his hostile words. She knew he was a dickhead, but the way he'd brazenly brought up her parents shocked her. But I guess it's not everyday someone with a perfect life runs into an *almost* orphan. Aloura decided not to give him the time of day, ignoring his harsh glare, she walked to the other end of the rooftop and leaned over the edge, watching the people below.

She silently prayed that he'd leave before the clock reached mid night, as she desperately needed to feel her heartbeat faster as she hung off the edge of the building. After a couple of moments of watching random strangers cross the streets below, Aloura turned to Elias and soaked in his features.

He was no longer in a suit, instead he wore a pair of tracksuit bottoms and a short sleeved black shirt. He looked somewhat sweaty, like he'd been on a run. His arms were muscular as they tensed on the railing, and bruises littered his knuckles. Elias felt the younger girls gaze on the side of his head, and he turned to her. Raising an eyebrow at her.

"You're hurt" she spoke after a moment of spotting the bruises and blood on his face. Elias fought the urge to scoff and sarcastically mention how observant she was. Aloura sighed before reaching into the small bag she'd discarded on the floor. She picked up the first aid kit and hesitantly walked closer towards him.

It was only when she was under the moons light did, he realises how beautiful she was. Her green eyes sparkled under his gaze, but he couldn't help but notice how dull she looked inside. *"How about that pretty lady you were with this morning?"* the boss' words replayed in his mind, taunting him. "Stay away from me."

"I'm just trying to help."

"I don't need your help." He growled, shifting his attention away from her and onto the street ahead of him. Aloura fidgeted with the first aid kit in her hand, and a frown on her face. What the hell was wrong with this guy?

"God you're such a pretentious, privileged arsehole" she growled back after a moment of studying him. She threw first aid kit to his feet before walking back towards her side of the rooftop.

Elias laughed bitterly, "I'm the pretentious privileged one?"

"Yes" she snapped back.

"So, you're so fucking privileged you don't even notice?"

"You have no idea what the fuck goes on in my life!" she reposited back, she dug out her phone from her pocket and looked at the time. 11:59. Elias knew he should have left it there, but his ego, and the fact he was already annoyed today pushed him to insult her more.

"What your mummy and daddy wont fucking buy you a pony?"

Aloura watched him for a moment, before she swallowed, "don't fucking talk about my parents." Her voice was low and hurt coated it. Elias knew he'd pushed it too far, but pride had made it impossible for him to apologise. Aloura watched the clock hit midnight, she closed her eyes sadly and turned to the city. Her mother's death anniversary wasn't meant to be a day of celebration- but she couldn't help but despise Elias for ruining the night.

Elias and Aloura settled in the silence, and after a few moments, Aloura started to swing her legs over the edge of the roof.

"Woah woah" Elias called out at the teenager, suddenly regretful for his words. He was only angry that he'd lost the fight and wouldn't get paid for another couple of days. He didn't want to be reason for someone taking their life. "Look I'm sorry- "

"I'm not going to jump, dickhead." She muttered the insult quieter than the rest of her sentence, but Elias still caught wind of it. He suppressed the urge to insult her back, reminding himself it was his tongue that got him in this predicament to begin with. "You just stand on the edge of the building and let go."

"And then you fall and die on impact."

"No-"

"You fall and you don't die, but you break your spine and you're forever paralysed" he cut her off again. "And then you're fucked because you can't even try again."

Aloura shot him a weird look before sighing at his dramatic antics. "No. you let go and the fear of falling reminds you how much you want to live." She swung her other leg over and looked down, Elias' heart beat in his ears watching her. "And for a moment, you pray. You promise whatever is up there that you'll stop complaining if you make it out alive." Aloura paused as she let go of the railing, "it reminds you how small your problems are."

Elias scoffed silently, *how small do your problems have to be so hanging off the edge suddenly fixes them.* "Look, little one." He sighed, "you need to find a better fix. What happens when one day this doesn't scare you anymore?"

"Then I jump" she joked, but she wasn't sure she was joking at all. She cleared her throat awkwardly, "I can handle myself. As you said, I don't need help."

Elias didn't reply, instead he watched her for a couple of moments, and she watched him. A brief moment of civilization between the pair. Elias walked to the discarded first aid kit and sat on his side of the roof and began tending to his wounds. Aloura watched him, unsure if this was his peace offering.

But she found herself fighting the urge to smile, accepting whatever peace offering it was.

Chapter Eight

Aloura and Elias sat on the rooftop almost all night. Elias wasn't sure why he'd stayed there as long as Aloura had. It wasn't like he enjoyed her presence, but the thought of leaving her hanging off the end of the building clawed at him from inside.

I wouldn't want Kalian out here all night alone, he'd convinced himself. He had only stayed because he saw the innocence of his brother in her. Yeah. That's all. All the while, Aloura wished on every star that Elias would go home. She wanted to cry, to talk out loud to her mother. She wanted to watch the sunset, without his lurking presence. She didn't mean to be rude to him, it wasn't her nature. But by 6am, she had gotten desperate for a break from his watchful eyes.

But Elias didn't move an inch from his place. His now bandaged hands gripped the cold metal bar bitterly. The thoughts of the fight filled his mind. He fisted his hands angrily and repeatedly hit his forehead, racking his brain for a way out of this life. Aloura swung over the edge and balanced herself back onto the building and walked to whcre Elias stood. "When are you leaving?" she asked him solely.

Elias shot her a look of disbelief, he had stayed up all night to keep a watch on her, and she was being rude? He scoffed, "when I feel like it.'

"When are you going to feel like it?" she pressed.

Elias ignored her question. Maybe he was unsure on how to answer her, or he was scared his tone would burn her more than he already had. But he let the silence between them linger for a moment, before turning to shoot her a quick glance. He opened his mouth to apologise for the way he'd acted from the moment he'd seen her, but Aloura's phone ringing phone cut him off.

Aloura took a step back from him, as she fished her phone from her back pocket, she missed the scowl Elias shot her direction at the sight of Kaden's name on her screen. "Hey babe!" Kaden called through the phone, and Elias' scowl deepened.

"Hey Kaden" Aloura smiled, she had missed him. They hadn't spoken since the night of his college party, but she had shook that reminder out of her memory. She didn't want to let her mind wonder to what had happened after she had hung up on him.

"Where are you?" he grinned through the phone.
"The rooftop, why?" she asked, picking at her nails anxiously. A habit she'd picked up from her mother.

"God's sake" he muttered under his breath. Aloura knew she wasn't meant to hear that, so she ignored it. "Hold still, I'm coming."

"What do you mean?" she rushed out, shooting a glance at Elias who had his arms off the building while he looked at the streets below. His jaw tensing angrily. "You're in Cambro?"

"Yes babe" he grinned, "I'll come to you now."

"No!" Aloura rushed out panicking as she stared at Elias. Kaden was, despite unfaithful, a jealous guy. Just the mere thought of Aloura and another guy interacting would send him into a rage. So Aloura wasn't looking forward to finding out how angry he'd get if he found out they'd spent the night together. *Despite how innocent the night was.* "I mean, don't bother coming all this way, I need to drop some things at home off anyway. I'll come to you." Aloura lied.

"Okay babe, my mum wants to see you anyway."

They exchanged I love you's and goodbyes, before Aloura turned to Elias, a smile still tugging in her lips. It however, quickly erased off her face as Elias scoffed at her. He picked up the discarded first aid kit and threw it at her hands, before walking towards the large door.

Aloura stood confused for a moment, she didn't understand how someone's mood could change that drastically in so little time. *You didn't expect to be besties just because he used your first aid kit, right?* The voice in her head scoffed. But Aloura sighed sadly, suddenly aware how desperate she was for a friend.

Aloura gathered her belongings before walking out the rooftop.

After a couple of minutes of walking, Aloura found herself outside Kaden's house. The excitement inside her bubbled up, pushing the sadness she'd felt earlier to the back of her mind. The butterflies in her stomach clawed at her throat as she spotted the familiar car in the driveway. Her face broke out into a smile as she practically ran towards the front door and knocked frantically.

After a few moments, the door swung open, and Kaden stood there, a smile matching Aloura's on display. Aloura wasted no time squealing and throwing herself into his arms. Kaden stumbled back as Aloura hung off his neck. "Hi there baby" he smiled, tightening his arms around her. "God, I missed your hugs."

"I missed you more" Aloura laughed in response before jumping out his arms. "Where's your mum?"

"You just missed her" Kaden sighed as he led Aloura into the kitchen, "she made us pancakes though, are you hungry?" he didn't wait for Aloura's answer before he began dishing out a plate for her.

"Yeah please, I've not had breakfast" Aloura grinned as her plate was placed in front of her. She took a seat as Kaden placed his food on his plate.

"You've not ate yet?" he raised an eyebrow, "I thought you were at the rooftop?" Kaden questioned, confused as to why she'd wake up at the crack of dawn and leave her house without eating.

"I went there last night"

"You slept there?" he exclaimed worriedly, "babe do you know how unsafe it is to be out alone all night?"

"I wasn't alone" Aloura's eyebrows furrowed, she stuffed another forkful of food in her mouth, before realising her mistake.

"Who were you with?" Kaden asked after a moment of silence.

"Just someone" Aloura mumbled. She was suddenly no longer hungry, and instead opted to play with her food. She had only ever made Kaden mad once before, and she certainly did not want a repeat of that night. He'd never hit her though, but the hurtful words he'd use sure did leave a mark.

"Was this someone a boy?" Aloura's silence was enough of an answer to Kaden,. He watched her for a moment, his eyes angry. "You just love doing what I tell you not too huh?" Aloura didn't look at him, she held her fork and messed with her food, waiting for his mood to cool down. But it didn't subside, her lack of response only enraged him more.

In one swift motion, Kaden's breakfast was thrown at the wall, Aloura flinched in response, but Kaden played it no attention. He jumped from his seat and paced around the table before stopping when he stood opposite where Aloura sat. "Were you with a fucking boy Aloura? Don't make me fucking ask you again."

"Yes but-" Kaden didn't let Aloura finish, he'd left the kitchen and angrily marched up the stairs, leaving his guest stunned in the kitchen.

Aloura followed Kaden up the stairs, and knocked at Kaden's now locked door repeatedly, "Kaden please" she called out. But Kaden didn't respond, and for almost five minutes Aloura stood at the outside of Kaden's door begging him to listen. She had begun to give up consoling him when the door unlocked, and a red eyed teary Kaden stood before her. He stood for a moment before swallowing. He held his hand out, and Aloura stepped hesitantly in his embrace.

"I'm begging you, Aloura please" he cried as he pulled her into his chest. Aloura wasn't sure what he was begging for, but she didn't dare question him, she instead wrapped her arms around him and promised him nothing happened again and again.

"Promise me Aloura" Kaden sniffed, "promise me nothing happened. Promise me nothing will happen."

Can you promise me the same, Kaden? She wanted to ask him, but again, she bit her tongue. The gratification she would feel from placing Kaden in his place wasn't worth the commotion it would cause. "I promise you"

I don't believe in promises.

Chapter Nine

Kaden's mouth pressed against Aloura's as soon her words died out in the air. His lips moving hungrily against hers, and she too lost in her hazy mind to process his actions. Why had she felt like she was lying promising nothing would ever happen? Every time she had seen him they had argued. Kaden pulled away for a moment and looked down at the girl lost in her thoughts. "Kiss me back Aloura" he whispered to her, his breath fanning her lips. She blinked for a moment and looked up at him. "Kiss me back" he repeated.

Aloura wordlessly pressed her lips onto Kaden's, standing on her tip toes to do so. Kaden smiled into the kiss, and Aloura could practically taste the saltiness of his now dry tears in the corners off his lips. Kaden's rested his hand on Aloura's right cheek before desperately speeding up his movements. Almost like he was fearful the girl before him would vanish into thin air, or worse, change her mind. At least in his mind that was worse.

Aloura pulled away and gasped for air, but Kaden instantaneously pressed his lips back onto hers. Taking her ajar mouth as an invitation. His tongue slipped in between the slit of her lips and wrestled with Aloura's hungrily. He moved his left hand to the breathless girl's hip and pulled her into him, and Aloura feigned a moan into his mouth. Kaden removed his right hand from her face and dropped it to the hem of her shirt, pushing his cold hands under the fabric and through the restriction of her bra, but not unclipping it off.

He fondles her breasts firmly as his lips leave her mouth and press onto her collar bone, sucking her soft skin. Aloura forces out another moan, and he hurriedly repeats what he just did, in hopes of more pleasure stricken sounds to slip through the girls lips. But his touch didn't pleasure or send butterflies to Aloura's stomach, it sent a chill down her spine, and the feeling of his lips against her's sent bile up her throat.

 This kiss was nothing like their first kiss, this one wasn't sweet. This was desperate, drunken. you don't kiss a girlfriend like that Aloura thought, maybe a one night stand or a stranger. Maybe that's all she was to him now. A quick pit stop fuck when he was away from college. Kaden placed his lips back onto Aloura's, and his hands at the back of Aloura's thighs and lifted her up, before walking towards his bedroom.

He dropped Aloura onto the bed, and a small shriek left her lips as bounced on impact. Kaden hurriedly slipped his shirt off., and Aloura parted her thighs to make way for Kaden. He leaned down between them, pressing his lips into her mouth for a second, before pulling away. He moved his lips to her jaw before prepping kisses down her face, and onto her neck. His fingers found the buttons of her shirt and fumbled with them. He briskly went to pull it off her body, before her hand caught his wrist. "Can we keep them on?" she didn't want Kaden to see her bruised body, but parts of her knew she no longer wanted him to see her body at all.

"Why?" he breathlessly questioned, showing no form of halting the unbuttoning of her shirt.

"Kaden please" she squirmed desperately, shifting beneath him in an attempt to show how serious her request was. Kaden dropped her shirt and looked down at her with knitted eyebrows, silently questioning what had gotten into her. When Aloura offered him no explanation, he sighed but complied, instead unbuckling his own jeans as she pulled off her tights.

Their lips found each other's again, and Kaden's hand pulled down his boxers as he positioned himself between Aloura. He grasped out his dick and turned to the girl who watched him with distant eyes. He jerked it off a couple of times as he watched Aloura, it was hard and angry in his hands as he spread his pre cum down his shaft before pulling a condom out his nightstand and slipping it on. Aloura closed her eyes as he positioned himself in Aloura's entrance, and with no warning he pressed himself deeper and deeper into her.

Aloura couldn't help the sadness that grew inside her, how was she so physically close to Kaden, but felt like there were miles between them. Even the sex wasn't the same.

The first time they'd fucked, he was gentle. His hands traced her body again and again. Almost like he was fearful of forgetting it. So, he'd repeated it to engrave the feeling in his memory. So, his hands felt full even when Aloura wasn't in them. He kissed her slowly that night, told her he loved her. Asked if she still wanted this- whatever this was. But this time as he slides in and out of her, his hands explore her body. Grabbing pieces and holding other repetitively- kneading Aloura's body into the silhouette he wished to fuck, a shape he'd become familiar with at college.

His hands looked for pieces of Aloura that didn't exist. "Fuck" he groaned, increasing the speed and space between them. The sound of Aloura's wetness filled the room as Kaden's balls repetitively hit her sex.

Kaden traced another's body onto Aloura's skin, a mould of another he wished the girl beneath him could fill. "Fuck, Amriss-" he groaned, his hands gripping Aloura's hips in place. Not pausing as he caught his words. "Aloura I'm so-"

Aloura's mouth felt dry, and her throat constricted. She watched Kaden as he continued to rock in and out of her as he mumbled out a string of apologies. "Just hurry up" Aloura cut him off sadly, she placed her hands on her face as Kaden watched her with wide eyes. he didn't have to be told twice, he'd quickly finished and rolled off Aloura.

"Did you finish?"

No. "Yes."

Kaden nodded and slid the used condom off, before typing it and throwing it into the bin by his desk. Aloura sat up, tear stains littered her cheeks. She watched as Kaden cleaned himself, too ashamed to spare Aloura a glance. She wondered what parts of Amriss he saw in her.

If he loved the parts of her that didn't remind him of Amriss.

"Babe-" Kaden turned to her.

"I have work." She didn't. Kaden knew she didn't, but he didn't press her.

Aloura cursed herself for not stopping him the moment his lips parted for whoever this Amriss chick was, but she wanted him in any way she could have him. Watching him moan another's name was more comfortable under him than away from him, anyway.

So, she sold herself short again, and took what he gave.

Chapter Ten

Aloura pressed her face deeper into the pillow as sobs racked her body, the moments she'd wished to forget replayed like a broken record. She scrunched her nose at the sound of him moaning for another. She'd always known he wasn't faithful- that was not what had surprised Aloura. It was the way he'd easily mistaken her for another- was she not special?

Parts of her had believed he'd only cheated because she was a far from him. That he imagined her as he fucked the others, not the other way around. Not that it made his cheating any more tolerable if he'd imagined her. But Aloura had too much on her plate to care about dumping Kaden. Plus, her mother approved, and that was all that mattered to Aloura. She had someone in her life that her mother had met. Maybe Aloura was just scared to change and grow out of her past, because that was the only place her mother lived.

Her heart couldn't handle another rejection. She wanted Kaden; she knew that much. So as a feeble attempt to mend her broken heart, she filled her mind with the happy memories they'd spent together. Reminding herself of the moment they both shared with her last mother, but the images of how carefree her mother once was saddened her even more.

Aloura was too engrossed in her mind to have noticed the time pass. They say time flies when you're having fun, but she wouldn't have called *that* fun at all. It wasn't until her father called for her did she realise she'd gotten herself fucked. Again. She lifted herself up from the bed and smoothed down her clothes, before wiping her tears.

She grabbed the broken mirror from her drawer and held it to her face. Her eyes were puffy, and if her dad wasn't pissed out his mind, he would definitely realise. She flinched slightly as his voice called for her again. She placed the mirror back from where she'd retrieved it, before walking to her door.

She had made sure to close the door after her; it was her safe haven, and although it wasn't necessarily the best of rooms out there, it was hers. And it was the only place her father did not destroy. She walked to the staircase with heavy feet, and a racing heart. She had not cleaned nor made dinner- all thanks to Kaden.

Aloura shook her head at the thought, she couldn't blame him, this was all her own doings.

"Seems like you've grown a backbone." Michael's words left his lips before Aloura even had the chance to step into the room. Aloura didn't reply, so he continued. "I let you off nicely last night." He told her, although Aloura couldn't remember him being nice at all. "And it seems you've now taken me for granted."

Aloura once again didn't reply, she knew better than that. Michael looked at his daughter, "why isn't my dinner ready, and whys the house a mess?"

Because you've not made it, and you trashed the house. Aloura swallowed what she really wanted to say, instead mumbling out a pathetic sorry, "I forgot sir."

He narrowed his eyes at her, "you forgot?"

Aloura nodded and blinked the tears that threatened to spill. She was never good at confrontations. She learned once in psychology class that she cried during arguments because when growing up she was never given the space to talk her anger freely. And Aloura connected to that.

"I ought to' teach you a lesson, maybe next time you won't forget." The lump in Aloura's throat grew at his words. He wasn't that drunk, which meant this beating would last for longer, and his hits would be more precise.

Aloura cowered away as he stepped closer, her eyes wide and breathing rugged. All she wanted was to be given a moment to feel her emotions. But it seemed like the universe, or whoever was up there, clearly had different plans.

Aloura heard the echo of the slap before she felt it.

Her father's nostrils were flared, and his teeth clamped shut when she'd looked at him again. Yet his eyes were the same, as cold and distant as the first day he stumbled in drunk.

That night was the first of many nights she spent on the kitchen floor. Laying in her own blood and tears. Except that night, she'd hoped her father would stumble across her in the morning and realise what he'd done.

It was safe to say he didn't care about what he'd done.

And that was the first time her father had broken her heart.

"Are ya fuckin' listening?" He snarled at her, Aloura blinked twice and nodded her head. Even though they both knew she wasn't. "You weren't raised right" he snarled; his hand fisted a handful of her hair. He pulled at it as he spoke, "Ever been told lying is wrong?"

Aloura didn't reply again, because she knew it was one of his old set ups. If she'd said she had been taught that, he'd have beat her for not following his teachings. But the opposite wasn't a better choice; he'd use the excuse that he'd teach her now, and thus, beat her. Not that not replying would get her out this predicament- but it was the lesser of the three.

"I fucking asked you a question" he slurred, tightening his hold on the girl. "So ya answer me. Got it?"

Aloura attempts to nod, but the firm hold her father had on her hair hindered her from doing so. Michael pulls Aloura's face to his and snarls at her, before dropping her. His foot meets her face and then her stomach before she has time to realise she was on the floor.

But he ignores her cries of pain and the blood that spilled into her hand as he steps over her limp body. "Don't dirty my floor," he tells her. "And I already ate, don't make dinner."

Aloura resisted the urge to lunge at her father, he had just lectured her, and hurt her over not making dinner. Yet he had just admitted to already eating. Aloura watched his retreating boots until they disappeared before lowering her head into her arms and letting her tears fall.

She wasn't sure why she cried. She was practically used to his treatment; it was basically a norm at this point. But she couldn't shake the feeling of disappointment that filled her every time. Although she wasn't sure if she was disappointed at him, or herself for once again indulging in the idea that people could change.

Chapter Eleven

Aloura found herself on the way to the place she seemed to find herself at every night recently, except this time every step was agonising. But she suppressed the pain, fearful others around her would notice what her father had done. She clutched her phone and her first aid kit tightly as shots of pain hit her stomach.

She'd finally made her way to the top of the cold staircase, and the blue large door came in her vision. It was left ajar. *Weird,* she thought to herself, *maybe Elias found his way here again?* The thought of sharing the rooftop with him again didn't anger her this time, she found herself picturing a shooting star and wishing on it that he was on the other side of those doors. Not that she liked that pretentious arsehole of course. But company was nice sometimes.

 She paused a few feet away from the steps, composing herself to be greeted by Elias, when a voice called from behind her. Aloura flinched and turned to face the lady she occasionally ran into. Aloura figured that she lived in the apartment complex, because her clothes were always casual- slippers and tank tops kind of casual. Aloura held the urge to roll her eyes at the sight of her.

She knew a lecture would soon spew out her thin cracked lips and bounce of the walls, entering Aloura's one ear and out the other. "The door is broken." She grumbled, "don't lock it from the outside or you'll get locked out there. I won't come to help you." And with one cold glare, she shut her apartment door in Aloura's face. Not giving the injured brunette time to question what broke it or thank her for the warning. Not that she'd have the guts to do either.

Aloura nodded to the now shut door and walked towards the broken rooftop door, pushing it slightly and taking extra care not to accidentally close it behind her.

She made her way to her favourite corner and laid her coat onto the floor before sitting on it. Aloura placed the first aid kit in front of her and opened the case. She was running low, and she knew she'd have to choose between food or restock of supplies this week. She rested her head back on the wall, the memories of Kaden moaning Amriss' name made her eyes sting. Aloura closed her eyes sadly, unwilling to give Kaden and his flings the satisfaction of her crying. She didn't know how long she stayed like that, but a few moments later light snores left her lips. A few rare moments of silence and peace she cherished in her life.

But it was soon cut short as angry steps made their way up the stairs and onto the rooftop, followed by the door slamming shut. Aloura gasped and her eyes shot open. She scanned the rooftop for a sign of her father, and when she found no presence of him, she sighed in relief. Her relief quickly was diminished as she narrowed her eyes at the now locked door and the culprit pacing around- unaware of her presence. At first, anger bubbled inside her. He had locked them up here, now she'd be late tomorrow and receive another beating, but as she zeroed her gaze at him, she noticed his injuries. The anger shifted to concern. She lifted her injured body off the floor and made her way towards the oblivious older man. "Elias?" she called out to him softly as she made her way to him. "What happened to you?"

Elias turned to her, his bruised fists locked, and jaw clenched. Aloura's advancing figure gave him ample time to scan Aloura's appearance. She looked a lot more dishevelled than the last time he'd seen her.

"I could ask you the same thing." Elias' eyes focused on the blood on her lips.

Aloura ignores his concerned gaze, and she moved her hand and reaches out for him. She placed her smaller hand into his larger one. Not missing the bruises and dried blood that coated them. Her heart clenched at the sight. She wasn't queasy, the injuries on him weren't the most severe she'd seen- she'd nursed worse ones on herself, but the thought of him being in slight discomfort didn't settle well in Aloura's stomach.

Elias' minds span the same thoughts. Cringing at what could have bought harm to the *privileged brat* ahead of him. He didn't like her, but he couldn't stand the thought of her being hurt. He swallowed as Aloura placed her hand gently into his, and he held it a little tight for a moment, as if he couldn't believe what his eyes could see. He loosened his grip, and was cautious not to ball his injured hands into fists, fearful he'd hurt Aloura by doing so. Aloura was aware of this, but only her bloodied lip was visible to him. She wondered what he'd do if he saw the bruises that littered her legs and ribs.

They made it to the small corner Aloura had made herself comfortable in, and Elias hesitated before taking a seat beside her. Mindful of how small her coat was, he double checked she was completely sat on it before sitting on half. Not caring he was dirtying his own clothes by doing so or the fact he was basically sitting on the cold concrete. "I'm running out on supplies." Aloura laughed nervously, "not that I'm always injured or anything." Elias lips tugged up into a soft smile as Aloura stumbled over her words. Cringing at the way she couldn't lace a full sentence together. She settled with a small 'anyway', before silence welcomed them.

She reached for his now discarded hand and placed it between them. She didn't miss how perfectly in fit around hers. But she shrugged the thoughts off, *I have a boyfriend-* she thought before frowning.

Did she?

Elias watched her calmly, the way her eyebrows scrunched together was adorable to him. But he didn't let that thought linger. He was dangerous, and dark. A sadist. She was pure. He didn't do adorable, and she didn't do dangerous. *She has a boyfriend.* He thought, before scoffing silently. *I don't give a fuck about your boyfriend little one.* He thought to himself. In fact, her having a boyfriend made him want her more. He shook these thoughts off again. He didn't want her at all.

Elias and Aloura were drawn out their minds when Aloura accidently applied too much pressure onto Elias' bleeding wounds. Causing him to draw in a breath sharply, and her to flinch at the sudden sound. Elias frowned down at her reaction as she pushed the feelings of anxiety that clawed her from the inside.

Aloura felt his gaze on her face as she carried on cleaning his hands, but she paid him no attention. His hand left hers after a moment and rested on her chin gently pushing her head up. "what's on your mind?" he asked, barely above a whisper.

Aloura panicked, unsure on how to word *I was thinking about how our hands fit together like they were sculptured as one and then broken apart* in a way she didn't make her seem like a creep.

Her forest eyes found his ocean like ones, and in the same quiet tone she spoke back.

"we're locked up here."

Chapter Twelve

Elias didn't reply to Aloura, and she couldn't help the sadness that bubbled in her stomach. She stubbornly, however, refused to admit it was disappointment she was feeling. Instead, she pinned it on anxiety. They were after all sat Criss crossed at the top of a twenty-story building, barely feet apart. She didn't even know the guy. Plus, he seemed to have a staring problem. It was only a matter of time before her introverted self-felt out of place.

Aloura had gone back to aiding his wounds after a moment of silence, and Elias continued to watch her delicate hands holding his rough ones gently. It almost made losing another fight worth it. He'd get hurt a hundred times if the scene before him was one that he could watch every time. "You need to start being careful. Did you get in a bar fight?" Aloura asked after she'd finished sterilising down his hands.

"I don't do bar fights sweetheart."

Aloura felt her stomach do a cartwheel and knock the air out her lungs in the process.

"Then why're you always injured?" Aloura questioned after her stomach settled.

Elias stared at her for a moment, before replying. "I'm a boxer" he didn't feel bad for lying, because he technically was. Except he had no say in it. And it was illegal boxing. Not that she needed to know anyway. *I don't owe her anything for helping me. We're basically strangers.*

Aloura held his gaze, as if assessing his words before nodding her head. "They don't have a medic for after?" she furrowed her eyebrows.

"No" *but even if they did, I'd much rather have you do it.*

"I can um bandage you up after again" she started, "only if you want." She added, in case he'd feel too pressured to decline her offer.

"Sure" Elias nodded a ghost of a smile tugging at his lips, he was thankful but unable to express how grateful he was to the younger girl.

"When's your next fight?"

"Tomorrow."

Aloura wanted to ask why it was so soon, he wouldn't even be healed from today's injuries. Instead, she nodded and pursed her lips together. Suddenly realising she was practically interrogating him. "you have-" she started, before she slowed her words down as she watched Elias' movements, "a cut on your cheek." Elias lifted his now bandaged hands to her lips. He ran his thumb over her cut and scrunched his eyebrows. He reached to the last disinfected wipe in the miniature box.

"What happened?" he asked, as he softly cleaned the dried blood from her bottom lip. Aloura didn't reply, instead focussed on her breathing. The fact he was that close to her, while speaking to her so softly, made her heart flip a million times in her chest. She resisted the urge to press a hand on her chest to calm it down.

"I have a bad habit of biting my lip." She lied, "and my nails." She held up her freshly bitten nails as if to prove to him what she was saying.

Elias seemed hesitant but he nodded as he finished cleaning her lip. "Bella-"

"Aloura" she cut him off.

"Hmm?" his eyes found hers.

"My names Aloura, not Bella."

"Aloura" he repeated, as if testing her name out for himself. Aloura almost passed out in his arms from the feeling she got from the sound of his voice uttering her name. "That's a beautiful name."

"Thanks, I- my parents, uh. They gave it me."

Elias' lips tugged up into a small smile at the sight of the stuttering girl before him, "weird" he joked, "my parents gave me mine too."

Aloura giggled softly, "that really is weird." She moved her gaze to the box before frowning. "You wasted a disinfectant on my lips."

"I didn't waste it if it was used for its purpose." He furrowed his eyebrows.

'It's a waste if it's used on me' Aloura wanted to argue. "But it was just my lip. I could have cleaned up your cheek!"

Elias didn't reply again. Just watched the weirdly attractive when angry girl that sat before him. He admired her eyes. He didn't have a favourite colour, but he knew he'd forever imagine her eyes when asked. "How old are you?" he questioned her after moments of silence had passed between them.

"Almost twenty" Aloura muttered. Unsure on why she said *almost twenty,* rather than nineteen. Maybe it was her bid to assure Elias she was old enough *for him, or whatever he wanted to do to her.* Nonetheless, she'd failed.

"You're a kid." He grinned playfully. Aloura shot him a glare.

"No, I'm not!" she whined, and Elias laughed in response. "Really I'm not!" she groaned after Elias silently shot her a look of disbelief.

"See you even act like a kid" he teased, finding humour in bothering the poor teenager.

"You're just a grandpa" Aloura huffed, unsure where her playful personality was coming from. Not even Kaden had managed to bring this side of her out of its shell.

"I'm not old!" Elias shot her a glare of his own. "I'm twenty-three."

"You're not even a grandpa" Aloura giggled, "you're a walking corpse."

Elias scowled in response, before Aloura cut him off again, a questioning look sketched in her face. "Did you just finish college?' Elias sighed sadly in response; his demeanour suddenly serious.

"No." he muttered bluntly, unwilling to offer an explanation. Aloura nodded, before Elias continued. "I never got the chance to go."

Aloura's eyes widened, she had never envisioned him as one to struggle; the first time she'd met him he was fitted into a tailored suit, with his black hair slicked back. In other terms- he looked rich. "Oh."

Elias muttered a small 'yeah' before redirecting the attention on her. "What about you?"

"I was set back a little." Aloura mumbled adverting her attention to her crossed legs, "but in a couple of years, ask me again!"

Elias' lips tugged at her sudden enthusiasm, or maybe it was the fact she'd indirectly assured him he'd earned a place in her life- even if it was for a couple of years. "What do you want to study?"

"Medicine" she grinned. "What about you?"

"I've never thought about going to college." Elias told her honestly. he was too busy stuck in the real world to have time to indulge in fairy tales.

'Well, think about it now." She grinned. He frowned a little thinking about his dream life. One where his mother wasn't sick, and Kalian wasn't miles away with a family they barely knew. But he couldn't envision a life lived for himself; but merely existing to assist the lives of others. "I'm not sure" he spoke after a moment. Sightly upset he didn't have a life plan besides surviving.

"That's okay. In a few years I'll ask you if you went to college" Aloura smiled at him reassuringly, adamant that both would one day live the life they'd dreamed.

Elias watched Aloura in return and nodded. Thanking her with his eyes with the words that felt too heavy on his tongue to speak.

Chapter Thirteen

Aloura had work again, but she seemed to be preoccupied. All her co-workers didn't miss the bounce in her steps, and the chirpy tone she spoke in- except no one knew why. Aloura was opening up again with Joe- and not even he couldn't manage to sour her mood.

Aloura had listened to him complain, or at least made it seem like she was, before nodding her head, smiling and offering him advice. Rather than ignoring him as per usual. Annie arrived later that day, and Aloura grinned as she heard the bell ring. "Annie!" Aloura cheered, throwing herself at Agnus' arms as soon as she'd stepped into the building.

"Bella!" Annie cheered in response, wrapping her arms around the younger girl. They held each other and swung for a moment. "I have something for you."

Aloura pulled back and frowned at Agnus. "You know I hate when you spend money on me" she told her.

Agnus nodded; she was aware of that. She had barely managed to convince Aloura to accept the free lunch that all the staff were entitled too. "I know Bella" she sighed, before reaching for her bag, "but this is different."

Agnus handed Aloura a brand-new book, the words 'I see colour' printed on the cover. Aloura didn't bother grabbing the book from Agnus before tackling her in another hug, muttering out a string of thankyous. "You're welcome, dear. Now, did you have lunch?"

Aloura grinned guiltily, Agnus shot her a frown, "No" she muttered.

Agnus sighed, throwing her bag onto a chair before lecturing Aloura. "What did I tell you dear? I told you that you must eat. Everyone eats! Its free food Aloura. I understand you feel bad but that's unacceptable. Honey..." she paused her lecture to turn to the girl that trailed awkwardly behind her. "Do you have an eating disorder?" Annie knew her question was out of line, but she couldn't help worrying. And now she thought about it, Aloura was in fact losing weight.

"What? No Annie. Of course, not" Aloura's eyes widened. "I'm just not hungry I promise."

"Then take it with you!" Annie cried out, "come on, I'll make you a take-out box that you can have later. Your shift finished ten minutes ago. Come on dear"

Annie didn't wait for Aloura to reply to her, nor did she check if she had followed her into the back kitchen. Aloura stayed in her place, sighing happily- grateful she had someone like Annie in her life.

Annie came back moments later, holding a takeaway box and a plastic fork. She handed Aloura the food and Aloura grabbed her belongings before checking out. "I'll see you tomorrow baby. You better eat!"

"Thank you, Annie," Aloura smiled, and held up the book, "and thank you so much for this."

It was only mid-day, and the night before Aloura and Elias had agreed to once again meet at the rooftop at midnight. It was hours away, but Aloura couldn't help the excitement that bubbled within her.

She made her way to the pharmacy, reminding herself to restock the now empty first aid kit. She'd have to go without food for a few days, but it was worth the moments she'd share with Elias on the rooftop.

She walked into the pharmacy door, smiling kindly at the technician behind the till. She made her way to the isle she'd found herself returning too every couple of months before gathering all she needed. She walked towards the till and handed them over.

"Hi again Aloura" Max, as written on his work tag, smiled. Aloura grinned back and mumbled a hi. "Is this all you need?"

Aloura nodded and grabbed the few notes she had from her bag. "That'll be twenty six dollars and fifty two cents please."

Aloura forced a grin and handed him the exact amount before taking her items and receipt and walking out the pharmacy, praying her father did not need a restock of alcohol for a while. Aloura made her way towards the rooftop, almost seven hours earlier than she'd agreed to meet him. Not that she was that excited, she just didn't want to risk her father coming home early.

The process of sneaking out, although she did it almost every night, was stressful. Aloura positioned her coat the same place she had the night before, before taking a seat and reaching for the book Annie had bought her. Excitedly breaking the spine, which was her favourite part of getting new books, before starting to read.

Hours had passed and it was already midnight. Elias had made his way onto the rooftop, catching sight of the sleeping bundled up girl in the corner. Her hands holding a book protectively to her chest, and a brand new first aid kit by her head. Elias admired the scene before him, a beautiful girl waiting up on him. He however, frowned as he noticed her head laying onto the cold concrete. "Aloura." He whispered, sitting down beside her. She didn't respond.

"Hey" he hesitantly reached over to brush her brunette locks from face. "Aloura"

Aloura shot up, scanning the rooftop frantically before sighing in relief as her eyes settled on the figure before her. "I'm sorry" he frowned, concerned. "I didn't mean to scare you."

"No, it's okay." Aloura smiled and sat up, rubbing the sleep from her eyes. Before turning to him and searching his face for any injuries, she looked up at him when she found none other than his knuckles and lip. 'Did you win?"

"Of course, I won." Elias grinned, "you're my lucky charm now sweetheart"

Aloura blushed at the compliment and adverted her gaze from him. She picked up the first aid kit in a bid to distract herself. Elias watched her with amused eyes as she fumbled with the kit before prying it open. His stomach filling with butterflies as she reached over and grabbed his hand.

"What time did you get here?" Elias asked after a moment of watching her aid to his cuts.

"Six" Aloura blushed, fully aware of the questions that would follow her confession.

Elias frowned. "You've been up here for six hours?"

"Yeah" Aloura laughed awkwardly, "I just wanted to read you know? but I fell asleep."

Elias didn't believe her. He fought the urge to ask why she didn't read at home but nodded instead. He knew too well the feeling of suffocation in your own home. The feeling of the walls slowly narrowing themselves into you, so he didn't push her. After all, we all need an occasional break from home. "What were you reading?" he questioned.

Aloura grinned as if she'd been waiting for him to ask. She held up her new book, Elias smiled and took it from her. "I see colour" he read the cover before looking back up at her. "What's it about?"

"A girl who lives in a world where you only see colour when you're in love" she gushed, "they've just introduced Auden"

"Auden?"

'The love interest" Elias nodded and stifled a yawn.

Aloura shot him a playful glare. "Am I boring you?"

"No, no" he rushed out. Suddenly panicked that he'd drive the young brunette away, "I've just not slept that's all." He wasn't sure why he cared about what Aloura thought of him; all he knew was he didn't want her to think bad of him.

Aloura frowned again and patted her lap. "Sleep now."

"Here?"

"Yeah" she grinned, "you can lay your head on my lap."

Elias thought about it for a moment before moving towards Aloura, "only if you read to me" He didn't really care if she read to him, but he saw the way her eyes lit up as she spoke about reading, and he wanted to sleep under the light of her eyes.

"Deal" Aloura grinned. "Oh, I saved you this" she handed him the lunch Agnus had packed for her. Elias frowned.

"I can't take that." He muttered, his head now resting in her lap as he looked up at her.

"It'll just get thrown away if you don't eat it" Aloura lied. She'd never waste food, but she desperately wanted to show Elias she cared *a little* about him; and her love language was gift giving. So, it was no shock she was offering him her last meal for a couple of days.

"Well, we can share it" Elias smiled softly, pulling the lid off the container, and digging his fork into the cold pasta. He lifted the fork to Aloura who had already began reading to him.

Much of the night was spent like that. Elias feeding himself and Aloura Agnus' now cold pasta, while laying on Aloura's lap as she read to him. When the food was finished, he discarded it beside him and laid back into Aloura's comforting embrace.

He closed his eyes, drifting in and out of sleep as Aloura's soft voice filled the rooftop, and her delicate fingers caressed his hair.

Chapter Fourteen

Aloura was the first out the pair to wake up. She let her eyes wander around confused as to where she was, and what the weight on her was. To her surprise, Elias had remained with his head on her lap throughout the night. The scene before her was heart-warming, but her mind was too hazy to appreciate it.

She grabbed her phone frantically and checked the time; eight in the morning. Her father was already awake, so she was sure to be limping for the next couple of days after he realised her absence. Aloura placed her hand over her heart to steady it, before focusing on her erratic breathing, but to no avail. Her panicked breaths filled the rooftop, and soon enough, strangled sobs racked her body. Elias woke up to the commotion, and as soon as his eyes settled on the panicked girl, he sprung to his feet. He had never consoled someone having a panic attack- but he had his fair share of them. He placed his hands in front of Aloura's face, a silent promise he wasn't going to hurt her, before moving them to steady her shoulders.

"Hey, hey" he mumbled grabbing her face in his hands softly, "it's okay baby, you're okay. you're okay."

When Aloura breathing didn't calm down, Elias shook her head softly in his hands, and ran his thumb soothingly on his cheek. "Can you name three things you can hear for me Aloura?" when Aloura didn't reply, he shook her again, "come on baby. Name three things you can hear for me."

"Uh" Aloura stuttered out, pushing past her erratic mind to list the things she could hear, "the cars"

"That's right hon, there's a load of cars. What else?"

"The birds" she muttered out after a moment, "and, and your voice."

"You're doing so good. Can you name two things you can see now?"

Aloura wanted to say she couldn't because the tears gathered in her eyes had made it almost impossible. But she pushed past that too and blinked them away erratically. "The rooftop, and you" her whisper was barely audible, but Elias smiled gently and nodded at her efforts. Aloura's heart flipped at his subtle reassurance.

"Last one sweetheart. One thing you can feel"

Aloura thought for a moment, before her face flushed red. Her eyes met his before she whispered, "your hands."

Her heart now raced for a different reason.

Elias smiled and nodded softly. Their eyes held each other for moments passing, before their gazes got lost in each other, and Elias found himself leaning in softly. His eyes flickered from her eyes to her lips, and Aloura let him, she gulped in excitement, before reality caught up with her.

"Uh I uh... have a boyfriend. Kind of" she muttered to herself more than him, but he caught her words, and chose not to press her further for information. Aloura almost grew disappointed when Elias pulled away. She wasn't sure why she had bought up Kaden, she didn't care if she kissed Elias before ending it with Kaden. He deserved that much.

I don't give a fuck about your boyfriend. Elias scoffed in his head at Aloura's words. *The only thing stopping me from kissing you right now is because you don't deserve to be sucked into this life I'm leading.* He desperately wanted to tell her, but instead, he nodded his head and forced a smile before kissing her cheek. "Yeah, of course."

Aloura smiled softly and got up before dusting her clothes off. She began gathered her belongings as Elias watched her, questions about what caused her panic attack hanging off the tip of his tongue. Aloura kept herself busy, refusing to meet his stare. Knowing he'd somehow find the courage to ask her what had happened a moment ago if he saw the glint of trust in her eyes.

"Sorry about that by the way." She muttered nervously; Elias nodded at her.

"I won't ask, don't worry" he smiled softly, as if he could read her mind. "Somethings are better left unsaid anyway." Elias knew that all too well. Aloura beamed at him thankfully.

"Thankyou" she launched herself into his embrace and wrapped her arms around his. Elias was taken a back for a moment before he returned the hug. Unbeknownst to her how long it had been since he'd received a loving hug. Aloura almost sighed in content with how safe his arms felt- but she bit her lip instead. "When's your next fight?" she asked then paused, "unless you don't need me too- "

"Aloura what did I tell you yesterday?' Elias smirked cutting her ramble short, "you're my lucky charm now sweetheart. I'll always need you."

"Then you'll always have me." She told him.

Elias smiled softly at her as she pulled away, and Aloura felt her mouth grow dry. She cleared her throat and motioned to the large blue door behind her. "I should" she muttered, pointing to it.

Elias nodded, "uh, before you uh go." He stumbled over his words. He lifted his arm and rubbed the back of his neck awkwardly. "Can we exchange numbers?"

If Aloura had smiled harder, she would have ripped her mouth open. She nodded excitely and fished her phone out her pocket before handing it to him. They exchanged numbers, and Aloura could barely tear her gaze away from her screen from excitement. She now had five contacts, one being her dead mother and the other her drunk father.

Aloura could not wipe the smile off her lips the entire journey home, she had made a friend. Or more than a friend. Someone who enjoyed the rooftop as much as she did.

But her happiness was short lived as her home came into view. She swallowed her thoughts and with shaking hands, unlocked her front door hesitantly. Her father's car wasn't in the driveway, but that wasn't enough reassurance for Aloura. He could have easily gotten a lift home- or in a drunken state, wandered home without the car. But after a few moments of pure silence in the house, Aloura's shoulders released the tension as she sighed happily.

Aloura made her way into the dirty household. The familiar stench of alcohol and cigarettes permeating the air. she sighed; fully aware Michael was expecting her to clean the mess before he returned this afternoon- preferably before she left for work.

♡ ♡ ♡

Aloura watched the clock anxiously as she dried off the last plates and placed them in the cupboard. She had ten minutes to make it to work, or she would be officially late- for the first time ever.

Aloura knew there would be no dire consequences for her tardiness, but the thoughts of somehow taking advantage of her Annie's kindness left guilt bubbling in the pits of her stomach. She dropped the tea towel into the washing basket and ran towards her room in a bid to change into her uniform and leave.

But at the sight of her mother's notes discarded on the floor, the guilt and anxiety of work was long forgotten. Aloura crouched beside the pile of papers she stole and picked them up.

Her eyes scanned the ink that lay on the sheets of paper, before stopping at the sight of her name scribbled hastily. *Aloura can never know. Aloura is safe.* Aloura's eyes scanned the words again and again, in search of a hidden message but after a few moments she came up empty handed. Her eyes followed the top of the sheet, *Michael knows I know.* Aloura cursed her mother vague writings- suddenly desperate to figure out the secrets her mother took with her to her grave. She held the other sheet of paper up.

Delivering you too evil

Aloura's eyebrows scrunched up in confusion. She fished her phone from her back pocket and opened the safari application.

She typed the words in and watched as the application spewed out different articles.

Aloura's finger pressed onto the first article.

> Underground world of crime leaves police chief stunned.
> "We're at a loss on what to do" the chief policeman told our LCT reporters, "all leads seem to be a dead end" he went on to say, "this is no ordinary criminal. This is a powerful organisation." When pressed for more information the chief told us about a recent attack at the police station.
>
> "Just last week they were taunting us. They spray painted their slogan onto the side of the building before wiping our camera's clean."

Aloura frowned once again and scrolled down the page to the attached photograph. Aloura eyes widened. The side of the police building graffitied with words that made her heart drop to her stomach.

Delivering you too evil.

Two devil like horns drawn above the evil.

what are you doing with these people mama? Aloura pleaded the skies silently but was pulled out of her thoughts as her phone rang.

Annie.

Aloura gasped and answered the phone, the dire situation at hand slipping from her mind as she frantically apologised to her manager for her tardiness. "I'm so sorry Annie. I'll be there in ten I promise and I'll stay behind-"

Aloura's rambles were cut short again as Agnus' voice reassured her through the phone. "Nonsense dear" Annie laughed, "you're never late so I got a bit worried about you. Take your time Bella."

Aloura thanked her old friend repetitively before ending the call. She looked at the papers in her hand and cursed them again. "Look what you've done!" she sighed as she lifted her mattress and placed the sheets under it. "You've made me late."

Chapter Fifteen

"Thank you so much for dining with us today" Aloura smiles at the couple as they placed her tip into the tip jar and walked out the building. It was only when no one was in sight did she sigh exhaustedly.

Although she slept on the rooftop, her bones felt achy and her mind fuzzy. She wanted nothing more than to crawl into her bed and lift the covers over herself and forget about the world around her. The problem with that was the world didn't wait for those who needed a break from it.

Aloura grabbed the wet towel and made her way towards the dirty table. Joe was working again today, but the word working could be used lightly. Unless you considered taking ten minuet bathroom breaks every five minutes was hard work.

"It's like he's basically getting paid to piss!" Cassidy, her other co-worker cried from her table as Joe made his way towards his tenth bathroom break.

Aloura didn't reply, he was leaving soon, she told herself. Just be patient. Plus, it wasn't that busy today. Instead, she began to gather the discarded cutlery and dishes into one large pile. The door ringing cut her off.

She, like every other one hundredth time snapped her head to the door. She wasn't necessary waiting for *someone;* that someone being Elias. Or at least she didn't think she was, but she'd saved him her dinner again and couldn't wait to give it him. She couldn't help the disappointment that filled her body as she found Kaden stood at the door instead. His tall build scanning the room for the sight of the brunette, green eyed beauty.

Upon spotting her shocked figure, he frowned and walked towards her. "I've been calling you."

"Yes, I know. I've been ending the calls on you." Aloura wasn't sure where this newfound confidence came from, but she liked it. She had never argued back with Kaden. Instead Aloura followed in her mother's footsteps of never taking too much room- because being small enough to fit in a man's hand meant he'd always have space for you. Kaden on the other hand didn't appreciate her newfound back bone, he couldn't believe his ears. He knew he'd fucked up- but Kaden fucking up *and fucking other girls* was a norm in their relationship. So why was Aloura not used to it.

"Aloura what the fuck" Kaden growled, grabbing her arm and forcing the girl to look at him. "Why have you been ignoring me?"

Aloura wanted to scoff, but she'd gained the customers and her co-workers disapproved and concerned glances. Aloura snatched back her arm from his grip. "Not at my fucking workplace Kaden."

"Why have you been ignoring me Aloura?" he growled again, ignoring her last statement. Aloura raised her hand to her head and rubbed it harshly. Unsure on how to put *you fucked me and moaned another's names* into words he'd understand.

Aloura once again looked around the room, suddenly uncomfortable as everyone continuously glanced at them. "Let's go outside and talk about this." She mumbled and stepped aside from him, leading him outside the bakery and round the corner.

"So?" Kaden called after her when they'd stopped walking.

"So, what Kaden?"

"So why have you been ignoring me Aloura. Don't play dumb." Kaden scoffed. Aloura found this ironic.

"I'm not the one playing dumb Kaden. Weren't you the one who fucked me, looked me in the eyes and called me another bitch's name?" Aloura's voice was sharp, and if Kaden was any closer, it would've cut him. Aloura found herself wishing he was closer.

"Oh my God." Kaden mumbled, "you're still on about that."

"What the fuck do you mean I'm still on about that Kaden?" Aloura snapped at him, using her finger she poked his chest harshly. "You fucking hurt me". Another poke. "I fucking loved you."

"It's been like three days Aloura. Drop it will you? It's my last day here." Aloura wasn't sure if Kaden was hearing what he was saying, but his insensitive words only angered Aloura more.

"How long would it take you to get over it If I fucked another-" Aloura didn't get the chance to finish, as Kaden, in an angered rage took steps towards her. In a swift motion, he slammed

Aloura onto the brick wall. Ragged breaths from the both filled the alleyway. Kaden raised his hand onto Aloura's chin and trapped her face in his hand, pressing down harshly. His jaw ticked.

"Don't fucking say that Aloura. I love you." Aloura didn't reply, instead she shut her eyes as tears filled them, she didn't want to cry for him anymore. Kaden on the other hand, let his flow freely. "Say it back baby" he cried. Aloura couldn't help but compare how the pet name from him made her feel different to the way Elias' did. "Say you love me too." His voice came out harsher, more desperate, and the hand pressing on Aloura's chin tightened.

Aloura didn't get the chance to reply to Kaden as he was ripped off her. She breathed in relief as she watched Elias hold Kaden by his shirt. Kaden was stunned for a moment, before his eyes darkened. "What the fuck do you want man?"

"You *never* lay your hands on a fucking woman." Elias growled, shoving Kaden with every word. "Especially mine."

The words that left Elias' mouth left both Aloura and Kaden stunned. Aloura's stomach filled with butterflies- no, elephants.

His words almost made her knees buckle beneath her, but at the sound of the two men arguing again, Aloura was snapped out her trance.

Kaden threw a punch at Elias, to which he returned- not stopping after one. Aloura stood for a moment shocked, before jumping into action. *He was going to kill him.* She grabbed onto Elias' hand and pulled him away from Kaden's now hunched over body.

"Is he the bitch from the rooftop?" Kaden growled at the stunned girl; his back was hunched over as he leaned against the wall. His face bloody. He spat some blood out before looking at Aloura. "That's who you're fucking?"

Elias growled and stepped in front of the silent girl, "don't fucking talk to her."

"Elias please" Aloura grabbed his sleeve, "let's go."

Elias offered Kaden one last scowl before placing his hand on the small of Aloura's back- a final blow at Kaden. Aloura's heart swelled at the subtle protective action, her skin heated at his touch. She was almost scared he'd be able to feel it through the thin material of her shirt. Elias kept his hand on Aloura until they'd reached the door, ditching it to pull the door open and motioning at Aloura to enter first with his head.

"Elias I'm so sorry" Aloura fumbled over her words, embarrassed he'd caught her at such a vulnerable moment.

"For what?" he mumbled, Aloura thought for a moment- she wasn't sure why she was apologising. She couldn't help but apologise- she'd been conditioned to avoid confrontation. To shrink herself so she'd fit in the palm of a man's hand. "he's the one who should be apologising. He had no right to touch you like that."

Aloura pursed her lips together awkwardly, unsure of what to say. She found herself losing the ability to speak around Elias more often than not recently. She looked at his jaw, a red tint now covering his stubble. "Does it hurt?" she asked softly.

Elias' eyes scanned hers, flickering between each eye. He lifted his head gently and clicked his tongue. He fixated his gaze once again at the golden specs in Aloura's eyes before dropping to her reddened chin. he raised his hand to touch it softly, caressing one side with his thumb. "Does it hurt?"

Aloura clicked her tongue and nodded her head slightly, the same way Elias had done moments ago. A grin plastered on her lips. Elias shook his head and smiled at the girl before him.

"Oh Bella! There you are. Cassidy told me you stepped out with Kaden." Agnus called from behind the counter. Aloura cringed- the memories of what had just commenced still fresh in her mind. "I ought to whip that boy's arse I tell you- oh Elias dear." She grinned and threw the towel onto the counter before making her way towards us. "How are you dear?"

Elias smiled gently at Agnus, "I've been great. You?"

"Great now that I've seen you with my Bella." Elias shot Aloura a confused look as she flushed red. "Not that I don't love seeing you here alone. But did you need anything?"

Elias' hand shot to the back of his head, rubbing his curls nervously. "I wanted to see if you had any more information flyers for the job vacancy."

Aloura's attention snapped to Elias, she suppressed the urge to squeal. "Depends on who's asking" Aloura joked, Elias faked a scoffed.

"Me of course"

"Then no" Aloura grinned. Elias laughed lightly, and Aloura caught the sound that left his lips. Embedding it into her memory; a sound she'd now replay when she's having a bad day.

"Oh, you love birds" Annie gushed, causing the pair to flush red and protest frantically- to which Annie ignored, obviously. "Yeah yeah" she sang, "why don't you two take a seat? I'll bring you some lunch."

Aloura opened her mouth to protest, but one death glare from Annie and Aloura complied, leading Elias to an empty booth. "So, you want to work here huh?" Aloura questioned after they'd settled from across each other. Elias nodded, "can you bake?"

"I used to bake with my mum all the time" he laughed, his eyes glistening at the memory of his late mother. Aloura's heart clenched in jealousy, before guilt swarmed her. *I don't have a right to be guilty that he has a mum* she scolded herself. "well- mainly she baked, and I licked every bowl clean" Aloura giggled in response. "What about you?"

"I wish" she spoke, trying to drain her voice of emotion- too scared to vulnerable. "I never have time. And I can't even If I wanted too."

"Why not?"

"I'd probably burn the house down. Last time I tried to bake cookies the oven exploded." Aloura cringed at the memory of the beating she'd received that night. "I think I was more upset about not getting to eat the cookies though." Aloura grinned.

Elias smiled at her fondly, listening to her talk about her memories was his new favourite hobby. Maybe it was because he loved the sound of her voice, or because of how carefree and happy she sounded talking about them. Regardless, Elias knew, in that moment, he would the rest of his days listening to these stories if she'd smile like this every time.

He hoped one day, she'd look at him the same way she looked at the stars the first night he saw her.

"Do you have a fight today?" Aloura suddenly asked, Elias shook his head.

"Not tonight."

"Oh" Aloura sighed sadly. She didn't mean for her emotions to be expressed so blatantly, but it was impossible to not be disappointed. Not that she liked that he fought, only the excuse it gave her to spend time with him.

"Oh?" Elias frowned, laughing lightly, "you like seeing me hurt princess?"

Aloura's eyes widened. "No! no. of course not" she rushed out, "I just wanted to go to the roof top. That's all"

Elias grinned at the suddenly shy girl, "then we'll go to the roof top baby"

Aloura's stomach flipped a million times.

Chapter Sixteen

Elias held the few notes he had in his hand. He'd won a single fight this week- and with the expenses he was paying on Kalian, he was tight on money. Had he been doing this from his own will, he'd easily make a couple thousand from every fight he'd win. But *the boss* took almost every single penny he'd earned. Leaving him to fend for himself.

Elias was tired of this life; he'd never had the time or effort to get a *real job*. The fights and training alone were enervating. He could barely pull himself together every night for a fight, let alone work during the day too.

But he'd realised he'd have to put his comfort last after he'd lost the two fights in a row- and the office job he'd initially applied for hadn't gotten back to him. He needed to pay his dads debts fast and get Kalian out of Italy. Just like he'd promised. But in the back of his mind, he knew he also wanted out this dangerous life for Aloura. Because he had never connected to someone as fast as he did with her.

Elias stuffed the notes into his wallet and entered the large supermarket- shopping list in hand.

butter, softened
caster sugar
plain flour
milk chocolate chips

He walked down the aisles; a concentrated look sketched on his face. He gathered the ingredients and made his way to the self-checkout till. Anxious he'd mess up the one thing he could do for Aloura.

He was never good at expressing his emotions- his father was a strong advocate of 'a man's manliness was measured by how hard he punched, or how loud he could yell.' But Elias always scoffed at that argument, more so after he took his life. How can one be considered strong when the only thing he could destroy was himself and those around him? Instead, Elias thought manliness should be measured by how much they could build or create- but his dad argued men would stand as nothing next to women. Which was Elias' point entirely.

Elias didn't want to know what his dad would think of him if he saw the *man* he was today.

♡ ♡ ♡

"Fuck me. Fuck you" he growled, collecting yet again another batch and discarding it in the bin, "and fuck this."

Elias hit his fist on the counter in frustration, he was on his third batch, and nothing was going right. He was frustrated and tired, and he had an hour and one last batch to turn things around. But it seemed like the universe was rooting against him.

He began taking his apron off in frustration before he paused, sighing sadly. His mind filled with Aloura, the way she'd clean his wounds with her gentle hands- how she'd save her dinner to share it with him, and how she'd offer him her lap to lay in as she read out loud.

He thought about how he desperately wanted her to feel the way she made him feel; *important.*

Even if it was doing something so miniature like spending the only money he had to bake her cookies. He wanted to do it for her.

Elias sighed, before re-tying his apron. He looked silly, Kalian made sure to remind him when he'd sent him a picture early that night. Elias grabbed the remaining ingredients, sighing sadly at the realisation that this had to be his last batch. *I'd better make it worth my money huh.* He asked no one in particular; a mere attempt to make the walls that surrounded him less cold. A figment of imagination where he wasn't alone.

Maybe one where his mother was with him, and his only job was to lick the bowls clean.

♡ ♡ ♡

Aloura sat on the bleak rooftop. It was once comforting, a place she'd once found herself retreating too. It was the highest building on the block- the highest she could access of course, but nonetheless, the closest she'd ever get to her mother.
She was sure her mother was watching down at her, but Aloura found herself wishing for more.

She wanted to talk to her mother; to tell her about Elias, how he made her feel the same way hanging off the rooftop did. She wanted to tell her about her father, and Kaden. How she didn't get to college. She knew of course, but I was different- Aloura wanted to tell her herself.

She desperately wanted to sit at her mother's feet and ask her to tell her the story of baby Aloura. How she cried for hours on end, and then never again. Truth be told, Aloura didn't enjoy that story much, but she saw the way her mother's eyes would light up when she'd tell her the story.

So, she'd sit, and watch the glint in her eyes, mesmerised with how loud her mother's eyes spoke to her.

Without Elias to share the rooftop with, it almost felt cold, like it was too large; the moons light didn't shine on the entire rooftop.

Aloura frowned as she watched the time tick on her phone, it was quarter past twelve, and Elias was late. She hated to be overbearing, but she couldn't help the excitement she felt. They had been religiously reading Aloura's new book together- and Aloura didn't want to start the next chapter without him.

"Do you like him mama?" she asked the sky as it glistened beyond the darkness. She wasn't sure why she asked for her mother's approval- Elias was merely a friend, and she hadn't had a proper conversation with Kaden about their lack of a future yet. "He's good to me." She added, in an attempt to convince her mother.

Aloura smiled at the memory of him calling her his woman. "Did you hear him earlier mama?" Aloura's mouth almost tore with how wide she smiled, "he called me *his woman.*"

Aloura was broken out her trance as breathless Elias made his way onto the rooftop. He wore a grey jumper, paired with a pair of navy tracksuit bottoms- a long shot from the clothes she first saw him in. Aloura scrunched her nose, "you're late."

"I'm sorry" he huffed, "I was um, I got" Aloura raised an eyebrow at his stuttering; she'd never seen him so *shy*. "I got caught up with something."

"With what?" she didn't mean to be nosy, but she desperately wanted to know what turned the six-foot giant before her into a stuttering mess.

Elias' ears burned red as he handed her the small container. "Are you blushing?" Aloura grinned as she stood up.

"No" Elias lied, although he could feel his ears and neck burning up. he raised his cool hands and pressed it on his neck, a feeble attempt to cool it down.

Aloura took the container from his hands and pried it open. The smell of freshly baked cookies permeated the rooftop. Aloura stared at the freshly baked goodies for a moment before adverting her attention to Elias. "For me?" she asked, barely above a whisper.

Elias' heart fluttered. He nodded. Aloura looked back down at the cookies. Tears prickled behind her eyes as her gaze met up to meet Elias'. Elias' eyes fell upon her tears and began to panic, unsure why his act of kindness was upsetting her. "What? No. Aloura" he rushed out; eyebrows now furrowed. "Don't cry"

Aloura's lips quivered. "This is the nicest thing anyone has *ever* done for me."

Elias smiled softly, his shoulders slumping in relief. "They're not much sorry" he ran a hand through his hair nervously. "I tried all night to make them perfect but-"

Aloura's eyes widened, "this isn't your first batch?"

Elias laughed awkwardly, "maybe it's my third" although his voice sounded more inquisitive than informative, "I lost count honestly." He mumbled.

Aloura's heart swelled again at the thought of him trying again and again for *her*. She placed the lid back onto the container, weary of keeping them warm for the both of them to enjoy while reading later.

After she was sure her cookies were safe, she turned to face Elias, swinging her arms around his body to encompass him into a hug.

Elias held her back, lifting her up slightly; prompting her to wrap her legs around his waist. Aloura laid her head in the crook of his neck, breathing in his warmth as Elias rocked them gently under the moons light; too comfortable to be the first to pull away.
If this is the reaction I get, he thought to himself. *I'd spend every paycheque baking you cookies.*

Chapter Seventeen

Aloura was situated between Elias' legs, her back pressed against his front as he held the book in her lap as he read aloud to them. Aloura had said she'd gotten breathless from the reading- but they both knew she just wanted to nibble on the cookies whilst listening to Elias.

Aloura would lift her cookie up to Elias' mouth every few minutes, and he'd take a bite, before continuing his reading. Aloura never failed to giggle at the sound of his voice muffled through his filled mouth.

They weren't sure when or why they'd agreed to the arrangement of sharing one cookie every time instead of one each- but neither of them was complaining. Elias thought the cookies tasted almost as good as when his mum had made them- but he agreed it was purely because he was being fed by Aloura. "Food fed to me by your hands tastes like heaven" he'd grinned at her after the first time she held the cookie to his lips.

Aloura blushed, and shyly offered him another bite.

"Have you lived in Cambro all your life?" Aloura asked, interrupting Elias from his reading.

Aloura felt Elias' nod from behind her, "what about you?

Aloura nodded too, "I hope to leave someday." *I'll follow you.*

"When?" Elias mumbled as he pressed his lips on the curve of her neck.

Aloura shivered in rapture, she forced her body to remain still and not push itself further into his embrace. "I'm not sure yet" she whispered, "do you want to leave someday?"

"I want to make a home somewhere- here or far. You just lead the way and I'll follow you" the words brushed past Elias' ajar lips before he could process the weight of them. Aloura smiled and leaned back in his touch. He wants to make a home somewhere, *with me.*

"What if I want to go to space?" Aloura joked, giggling slightly. Elias' lips tugged up against her neck.

"Then I'll build you a rocket fit for a queen."

Aloura's heart bulged in her chest, almost enough to leave a mark on the outside. She replayed his words again and again in her mind, her heart speeding with every scenario she pictured in her head. Aloura didn't reply, and Elias didn't need her too. He knew how much his words meant to Aloura- and he swore to speak kind to her for the rest of their lives, and to build her a rocket ship if she ever needed it.

Aloura reached her hand back behind her and pressed her hand into Elias' curls as he opened the book and continued to read out loud. Aloura's eyes fell onto the star in the distance blinking down at them. She giggled in her head, subtly pointing to the boy behind her. *Look mama.* She wanted to call out.
"What're you doing?" Elias laughed at the girl between his legs, Aloura froze, her face heated up at the fact he'd caught her. She turned around from Elias' hold to face him.

"Do you want to meet my mum?" she smiled at Elias, the question brushing past her plump lips before she could process it, her voice laced with excitement.

Elias' head snapped to Aloura's hopeful gaze; his eyes glistened earnestly. "Yes" he grinned before he could stop himself from answering. He had never met anyone's mum before- all his relationship had been random fucks. He liked it that way. Panic filled Elias as quickly as the sound of his voice died from the air. What if she didn't like him? She'd want someone who's not so messed up as her son in law. Someone like Kaden.

Aloura didn't give him time to back pedal his answer, she turned around, pressing her back into his front before she pointed to the sky. Elias frowned, following her extended finger. "Look" Aloura smiled as Elias watched the sky with a confused gaze, giggling at his expressions. "There look. That star that's blinking."

Elias' eyes widened as he'd realised the meaning of Aloura's words- her mother wasn't alive, and he had called her privileged and pretentious. Guilt bubbled in the pits of Elias' stomach. Suddenly understanding his mother's always *be kind* teachings. "Oh" he mumbled, his mind hazy with thoughts.

"I have her eyes" Aloura grinned, she turned around to Elias and opened her eyes wide- in case he had missed them of course. Elias laughed.

"They look beautiful" he smiled at her, adverting his attention back to the star that was now hard to miss. "Hey uh" Elias mumbled, reaching to rub the back of his neck awkwardly. "How did your mum uh die?"

Aloura almost flinched at the word choice- she knew her mother was dead of course, but pretending she lived in the stars gave her some type of solace. "Dad said it was a car accident" Aloura mumbled, watching the star ahead of her. Elias looked down at her, his eyebrows furrowed, and he nodded his head subtly. She almost sounded unsure- so Elias pressed further "your dad said?" he lifted his hand to touch the ends of her hair, playing with them as he watched her. "Do you believe your dad?"

Aloura shrugged- she didn't believe him. He had burnt her death certificate the second Aloura laid her hands on it. "The police showed up at her funeral" Aloura said after a while, "dad told them to fuck off" Aloura didn't directly answer Elias' question, but her words were enough conformation for him.

Elias nodded, his fingers tangled in the ends of Aloura's hair, "I bet she was beautiful" he tucked a few strands of hair behind her ear, although he couldn't see her face.

"I look like her" Aloura grinned,

"Then I know she was beautiful" Aloura blushed her eyes shooting up to the star that twinkled back down at her. *Did you hear that too mama? He thinks we're beautiful.*

"Thanks" she mumbled pushing the strands of hair Elias had placed behind her ear out. "What are your parents like?"

Elias breathed in, he dropped the hair he was playing with and watched the star Aloura had pointed out. He had never noticed how bright it glistened in comparison to the others, but now he'd never miss it. Elias ignored her question, instead, directing his own at her. "How do you know she's up there?"

Aloura frowned- she never knew why she thought her mother was living up there, she just felt it and went with it. "Mama said that one day she'll sit on the brightest star and wait for me."

Elias nodded, "is every star someone's loved one waiting for them?" he asked after a moment of searching the sky for his own parents. Aloura giggled and nodded. Elias smiled, his eyes fell on two stars that sat together, he lifted his hand and pointed to them, "then those are my parents."

♡ ♡ ♡

Aloura glanced down to Elias' and her intertwined hands for the hundredth time- smiling at the sight of them as butterflies filled her stomach. She had held hands with a boy before, specifically Kaden, but never in public. Aloura looked noticeably shorter than Elias as he led them down the dark deserted roads. It was a few minutes past five in the morning, and Elias was walking her home. She didn't need anyone to walk her home safely. The empty streets were safer than her home- but didn't dare breathe a word of it to Elias.

Aloura had just looked up from their intertwined hands for the hundredth and sixth time when she'd noticed a figure pacing outside her door. Aloura almost dropped Elias' hand to hold her stomach anxiously. It was only when they'd neared Aloura recognised Kaden's figure. Kaden paused and watched the pair making their way towards him, his eyes darkening at their hands. "What now you're a fucking cheater?" Kaden sneered as Aloura, and Elias stopped Infront of him.

"You mean like you?" Aloura retorted, holding Elias' hand tighter in an effort to comfort herself and calm Elias. She watched

Kaden who stood before her, Elias' previous work presents on his face. He was now sporting a split swollen lip and a black eye.

"Two negatives don't make a positive" Kaden ran his hand through his hair as he paced around.

"One negative wasn't a fucking positive either, so what's the difference?"

Kaden didn't reply to Aloura, unsure on how to reply to her. She was right, he'd cheated on her multiple times, but she chose to stay. It wasn't his fault. Right? She could have left if it bothered her that much. So instead, he turned his attention to Elias who watched the scene before him with dark eyes. "What happened to bro code?" he growled at the silent man.

Elias stepped forward in an intimidating manner, and Aloura was quick to raise her other arm and wrap it around his bicep. "I'm not your fucking brother."

Kaden took a step forward and Aloura stepped between them, giving her back to Kaden. "I'm just going to talk to him" Aloura spoke quietly so Kaden didn't hear. "I'll see you later, okay?" Elias frowned at Aloura's words and looked above her head.

Kaden stared at the scene before him with a clenched jaw, his eyes fixed on Aloura's hands on Elias' body. "Okay?"

Elias eyes found Aloura's. He nodded, his jaw tense. He raised his hand to Aloura's waist and placed a gentle kiss on her cheek. An assertion of dominance towards Kaden, and a form of comfort for Aloura. She blushed, "stay safe, okay?" Elias mumbled as he placed Aloura's hair behind her ear. "Call me if you need anything." Elias moved towards Kaden.

"One fucking strand of her hair gets touched and I'll have your head. Got it?"

Chapter Eighteen

Aloura folded her arms over her chest and blinked at Kaden who towered over her angrily. She was cold, tired and hungry, she wasn't in the mood to talk to Kaden. She found herself feeling like that a lot recently. She couldn't stand anyone, except Elias and Annie of course.

 "why're you still in Cambro?" Aloura asked awkwardly after a moment of silence. She didn't mean the question in a rude way, but it certainly sounded like it, so Kaden scoffed.

"What are you? A fucking migration officer? I can come and go as I like" he sneered, his voice hostile and his eyes dark. Aloura pursed her lips in a thin line and nodded, she wiped the sheen of sweat that covered her hand on her sleeves. She didn't mean to anger him already, but she could not think of a single thing to talk to him about. Kaden sighed, taking a step towards the anxious girl. "What happened to us Aloura?"

"You" Aloura frowned like it was obvious- except it was obvious. To everyone but Kaden it seemed. "Ever since you've gone to college you changed."

"Ever since your mum died you changed!" Kaden cut her off, his voice raising with every word he spoke. "You became distant. You don't come over or let me over!"

"Yes, Kaden it's called grieving"

"For how fucking long?" Kaden's words left his lips before he could stop them, and before they reached Aloura's ears, he began apologising. "Baby. I didn't mean that." Kaden's hands reached out for Aloura's shoulders who shrieked and stepped out his reach.

"Don't call me that." Aloura pushed his arms away from her body. Her shoulders now stiff and breathing laboured. It felt wrong for someone other than Elias to call her a term of endearment, even though technically Kaden was her boyfriend. Kaden's eyes followed Aloura's anxious movements in silence- and that only seemed too scare Aloura more.

"Kaden, we need to talk." Aloura spoke after a few moments of silence, her heartbeat rang in her ears in anticipation of his reaction.

Kaden didn't reply, but he stepped back and watched Aloura, so she took his silence as an invitation to continue. "I can't be with you anymore. I thought you were what I needed but I've now realised you're not what I need" Aloura watched her shoes, "or what I want."

Kaden's heart sank. He loved Aloura, in a weird way. But loved her, nonetheless. His *extra curricula* activities at college were nothing but one-night stands. He didn't see them as cheating, rather living the college life. "What? But" Kaden swallowed. "we've been together for" Kaden racked his brain but came up empty, "For so long."

Aloura smiled bitterly, "I thought we were meant to be."

"We are meant to be. Aloura I'm sorry."

"If we were meant to be, Kaden" Aloura sighed as tears filled her eyes. "Then we would have been. But were not." Her tears were not for Kaden, or the end of their relationships. But for officially outgrowing the girl her mother knew.

"So, this is it?" Kaden whispered, tears filled his own eyes and desperation laced in his words. "All for that bitch."

"Don't call him that" Aloura stepped into Kaden's face, she pressed her finger in his chest, "you don't know him."

"I don't know you either it seems. The more I get to know you the more I realise I don't know you at all" Kaden snapped grabbing Aloura's hand off his chest. "You never used to speak to me like this." He dropped Aloura's hand. "I don't like the version of you that he brought out."

"The version you can't control or manipulate?" Aloura laughed, she walked towards her doorstep, away from where Kaden stood. "If you want to play this way, have fucking fun with Amriss."

Aloura opened the door and slammed it shut in Kaden's face- forgetful of her hung over father a few meters away from her. Kaden outside kicked the fence angrily, he ran his hand through his hair a couple of times before walking down the now slightly lit street, angrily wiping tears that seeped down his cheek.

Aloura rested her back on the door, her breath laboured. Aloura lifted her arms and rested the heels of her palm on her eyes, rubbing her eyes and then holding her face. She stared at her feet lost in thought, but angry stomps down the stairs made her flinch.

"Who the fuck do you think you are walking in and out of my house at times like this?" Michael growled as he grabbed a hold of Aloura's arm shaking her with every word. "Where the fuck were you?" Michael's alcohol reeking breath fanned Aloura's face, and she shivered in disgust. "You've been selling yourself like some whore in the streets, haven't you?"

Aloura didn't reply, and that only enraged Michael more. His grip around her arm tightened, pulling her further into the house before dropping her frail body on the floor.

Aloura blinked away the tears as she watched her so called fathers every move, her arms wrapped around her head protectively as Michael raised his foot and brought it down to Aloura's body. But it wasn't the hits that shattered Aloura's world. It was his words between every hit.

"You killed your mother. Now you're gonna kill me."

♡ ♡ ♡

Elias lifted his arm and punched the bag that hung before him again and again. He was angry, he hated the thought of Kaden, but the thought of Kaden alone with *his almost girl* angered him even more. He knew it wasn't a good idea to leave them alone after their last encounter, but he didn't want to be overbearing or controlling.

Elias threw one last punch at the bag before stopping, he lifted his glove and wiped the tip of his nose, his eyes remained strained on the bag. Sweat glistened on his bare chest as he repositioned his feet and lifted his arms up at his face.

"Hello there pretty boy" a voice called behind him, Elias' head snapped to the door. His shoulders relaxed as Blayde's figure came to view. "You show up to training before me? Are pigs flying too?" Blayde laughs as he makes his way into the ring.

"Shut up arsehole" Elias mumbles humorously, he moves towards Blayde, and fist bumps him, before pulling him into a one-armed hug. He taps his back a few times and let's go. "I need to win." Elias spoke, determination coating his tone.

"Damn right you do, let's get started." Blayde walked to the corner of the ring and picked up a clipboard, "listen up pretty boy. Your opponent today is called Chase, twenty-one years young, five ten-" Blayde listed out as Elias chugged down water. Their attention was drawn away by Elias' phone ringing from the side-lines.

Elias looked at Blayde who sighed and nodded his head to its direction. Elias dropped the water bottle and walked to his ringing phone while pulling the glove off. Elias swallowed as he picked up, and disappointment bubbled when it wasn't Aloura on the other line. But his disappointment was short lived as Agnus voice filled his ears.

"Elias dear" Agnus' cheery voice called out, "you recently applied for a job here. Am I correct?" Agnus laughed, Elias laughed lightly too- he'd applied, everyone knew he applied. His *little scenes* with Aloura and Kaden were witnessed by basically everyone.

"Yes, ma'am that's right." Elias grabbed the ropes and pulled at them, unsure on what to do with his hands as he listened to Agnus' voice.

"Oh, don't call me ma'am. You make me feel old" Agnus joked even though she was old. "Anyway, I won't keep you for too long, can you start today? Joe's left earlier than expected and I need someone to cover with Aloura."

Elias thought for a moment, his fight was tonight. "What time?"

"It's a short one tonight. from three till six. If you can't I totally understand I called you such short notice-" Agnus blabbered, Elias could almost see her pacing behind the till and wiping her hands down her apron.

"No no- that's fine. I'll be there. Thankyou Agnus."

Elias ended the call and spun to a bored looking Blayde who had rested his weight on the ropes, looking down at the sheets of paper in a bored manner. "Fucking finally" he called out after he noticed Elias disregarding his phone. "Girlfriend?" he asked as Elias reached to him.

Elias shook his head and clicked his tongue, "new employer" Elias broke out in a grin, and Blayde's face matched his.

"No fucking way, someone actually hired you?"

"The fuck is that meant to mean dickhead" Elias laughed and grabbed Blayde's body, placing him into a headlock. Blayde had always been a fighter, with dreams of boxing as a career, but after a serious injury, he was forced to kiss his dreams goodbye. So, it was no surprise that he struggled to get out of Elias' firm grip. What surprised him was the familiar voice that called into the room. Causing Elias to immediately drop his best friend, or formally, his coach.

"Do I pay you to play fucking tea pots or train?" Elias' eyes widened at the person that stood before him, his head snapped to Blayde who looked stunned to see their boss too. "Blake. What is the meaning of this?"

The boss' physique was anything but intimidating- he was rather scrawny, and both Blayde and Elias towered over him. And if it wasn't for the power he possessed in the tip of his finger, Blayde and Elias would have seen to it to teach him a lesson of their own.

Blayde didn't reply to the boss, instead he watched him with wide eyes, his chest rising and falling from the wrestling session he'd had a few seconds ago. Elias turned to look at Blayde after he didn't reply, urging him with his eyes to say something, anything.

"Very well then, stay quiet. I'll just cut your pay." The boss' eyes bored into Blayde, before turning to look at Elias. "The both of you."

Elias' breath got caught in his throat. He couldn't make ends meet as it was, with a pay cut, he wouldn't even be able to afford rent, let alone Kalians too. Or food. Aloura's cookies. How would he make her cookies? "You can't do that." Elias growled taking a step towards the man.

The boss laughed, looking down at his pristine shoes before lifting his arm to tug at his tux. "Really?" he grinned. "I could do much worse."

Elias didn't speak, instead he bit down on his jaw and took a step towards the smug figure. Elias' arms instead went to his untarnished collar, he shook the man before him with every word. "No. you fucking can't." Blayde snapped out his trance and moved quickly towards the commotion, tapping his friends back and whispering a 'relax man.'

Elias' head turned Blayde's fearful face, Blayde's eyes widened a little, begging his friend to release their boss, before the situation escalated. Elias breathed out his nose and clenched his jaw before dropping the boss' bundled up shirt.

The boss grinned a little, fixing his collar and shirt, before stepping into Elias' face. His hand flew to the back of Elias' neck, his grip deadly. Their faces mere inches now, Elias could practically smell every meal he'd had in his life. "Step out your fucking place one more time, and it won't be you who pays" he warns, his grip tightening around Elias' neck. "It'll be your fucking girlfriend." Elias tensed as his eyes dropped to his boss' other hand which was discreetly finding its way into his blazer.

Elias struggled in his grip, but he just tightened his hand, pulling out a sheet and handing it to Elias. Elias frowned and took it, his shoulders tensing and his heart dropping at the sight of what was on the sheet.

A photograph, of him and Aloura, hand in hand. *This morning.*

"Know your place, Elias. Or the pretty Aloura West can be your reminder."

Chapter Nineteen

Elias frowned as he wiped down a table, his eyes periodically watching the door for Aloura. It was quarter past three; Aloura was fifteen minutes late, and Elias hadn't heard from her since he'd left her with Kaden. "Is she always late?" he turned to his new co-worker, Cassidy as she cleared the table next to him.

Cassidy placed the glasses in her hand and frowned at Elias before adverting her attention to the clock behind him. She frowned and shook her head, "almost never." She turned around and took the dirty dishes to the back of the bakery, leaving Elias with a pit of uneasiness growing in his stomach.

Minuets, which felt like hours to Elias later, and a dishevelled Aloura entered the building. Her eyes remained trained onto the floor, Elias was quick to move to her, placing his hands on her shoulder. She flinched back, and Elias didn't miss it. Elias frowned; she still hadn't looked at him. He turned to the fairly packed room and sighed before he grabbed her arm gently and led her to the back for some privacy.

Elias locked the door and turned to face Aloura who remained transfixed on her shoes. He sighed again and placed his hand gently under her chin, forcing her gaze to fall on his. His eyes darkened at the sight of Aloura's face.

Elias' thumb brushed over Aloura's bloody lip gently, before pushing her head further up to view the large red handprint littering her porcelain skin. Elias' hand guided Aloura's face to the side as he angrily eyed her injuries. "Who gave you these bruises Aloura?" his voice was soft but firm.

Aloura moved her face from his grasp and turned around without replying. "Aloura?" Elias called as she wrapped her arms around herself. she rubbed her arms in an attempt to rid of her goose bumps. But to no avail. "Aloura. Did Kaden do this to you?"

"No Elias. I fell."

"Bullshit" Elias yelled, his hand hitting the desk beside him, Aloura flinched into herself. Her eyes remained closed as the echo of his voice died down. "Aloura?" Elias called after a moment. His voice much calmer now. "Look at me please."

Aloura looked up at the pleading man whose heart broke at the sight of her tearful eyes. "Who hurt you?" Aloura shrugged.

"Who hurts you?" Aloura questioned him, accusation detectable in her tone.

Elias frowned. "What?" his eyes flickered between hers, his eyebrows furrowed together.

"You're always hurt too. You said you're a boxer, but no one fights at midnight. Unless it's illegal. So" Aloura stepped forward, "who hurts you?"

Elias scoffed and looked away, running his hand through his hair, "you have no clue what you're talking about Aloura-"

"So, tell me-"

"-I can't"

"Then neither can I" Aloura said, her tone final, and her eyes fierce. Elias watched her for a moment before pacing around her.

"God damnit Aloura. That's different." Elias stressed, he continued to pace around, and Aloura frowned at him.

"How is it any different?" she laughed bitterly, "you have secrets and so do I. I've respected yours and all I ask is for you to do the same."

Elias didn't reply, he turned to the wall and threw a punch- and Aloura silently thanked the universe no one was here to see the scene playing before her. Elias continued to face the wall, his breathing rugged and his shoulders slumped in defeat. Aloura watched him for a moment before hesitantly walking towards him. "Elias?" she whispered, her voice delicate, fearful if she spoke in any other tone the man before her would crumble at her feet.

Elias didn't reply, so Aloura called for him again. "Eli?'

At the nickname, Elias' head snapped towards the apprehensive looking girl. He had vowed to stay away from the young girl after the boss' threats today but hearing the nickname spilling out her soft lips made Elias lose all sense of judgement. Elias stepped towards Aloura, who stepped back, her heart beating so hard she was fearful its outline would be permanently etched on her chest.

"What did you just call me?" his voice low, his eyes dropping to watch her slightly parted lips.

Aloura's back hit the wall, she watched Elias with wide eyes, "Eli" her voice hesitant, and barely above a whisper. Elias lifted his hand and rested it on the wall beside Aloura's head. He inched his face closer to Aloura's. closing his eyes as the nickname fell from her lips again.

"The way your lips say my name makes me want to do things to this pretty mouth of yours." He ran his thumb down her lip, dragging her bottom lip down with his finger. Aloura's forest eyes watched Elias through her thick lashes.

"Like what?" she moved her face closer.

Elias' eyes flickered between her eyes and her lips. He didn't reply to her, instead, he slowly pressed his lips onto hers. Their eyes fluttered shut at the sweet taste of each other. Their lips moved in sync, and Aloura's heart fluttered as she felt Elias' smile through the kiss. Elias pulled away for a moment, breathing down at the girl in front of him. His eyes remained closed. Aloura pushed herself to stand at her tip toes, pressing her lips once again on Elias' who welcomed them happily.

Elias' teeth tugged at Aloura's bottom lip, and Aloura moaned softly into his mouth. Elias groaned as the sound of her rung in his ears, he pushed her back onto the wall, before using his hand to grip her waist and pull her into his pelvis. His tongue traced the slit of her lips, and Aloura opened her mouth silently, allowing him in. Elias slipped his tongue in, and Aloura whimpered into his mouth.

The door rattled open, and the pair flew off each other, turning to face a stunned Cassidy with beet rose faces. "Holy fucking shit" Cassidy laughed as she made her way to Aloura, examining her plump lips. "He kissed you so fucking hard your lip is swollen?" Aloura blushed at her words. Unsure if she should tell Cassidy her dad beat her or let her believe Elias had kissed her that hard. Cassidy's eyes widened at her handprint that sat on Aloura's cheek. "You have a slapping kink too?' she furrowed her eyebrows at Elias who was stood rubbing his neck awkwardly.

"What?" Elias rushed out. "No"

Cassidy pulled a look and rolled her eyes at the pair, mumbling a 'mhm', before turning to the door, "Anyway love birds. You should get out of here and you know, do your job?" Cassidy laughed, winking a Aloura before shutting the door behind her. Silence settled in the room, as the pair awkwardly watched the now closed door.

Elias was the first to break the silence, turning to Aloura and mumbling out an 'uh', and Aloura was quick to nod, despite Elias having not said much to agree too. "The kiss uh-" Aloura finished, it was now Elias' turn to nod. The pair settled in silence again before sharing a laugh. Elias sauntered towards Aloura, softly grasping her face into his hands.

His eyes fell to her bruises and darkened quickly. "No more secrets?" he whispered to her after a moment. Aloura stared up at him and smiled, her gaze fell to his hand as she pried it from his face. Elias frowned at her, "what're you doing?"

"It's a pinkie promise" Aloura laughed lightly, grabbing his bruised hand and prying his pinkie from his locked fists. Her heart almost dropping at the sight of a small tattoo on his forearm. *Evil* incised into his skin, with two horns resting above the words. She stared at it for a moment, before shaking her thoughts away. *I'm just seeing things. I'm tired.* Elias watched silently, before nodding his head.

"Now what?" he raises and eyebrow as his eyes lock with Aloura's.

"You wrap it around mine" Aloura's gaze fell back onto their hands. Elias continued to watch her, and Aloura could feel her hands tremble from the nerves. His gaze almost burnt her, but she refused to meet it. "Just like that" she grins, gesturing to their now locked pinkies. "Now the promise is sealed in." Aloura's voice begins to falter. Elias' eyes fall to Aloura's lips. She licks them, and his eyes darken.

Although they'd already kissed, Aloura found her knees beginning to weaken, and the oxygen around them no longer enough for two. Aloura's eyes flicker between Elias' and they stay like that for a moment, both too scared to be the first who pulls away. "That's all?" he whispers after a moment. His eyes now remaining on her lips.

Aloura swallows, but nods, not trusting her voice to speak. "You can't break it" she whispers after a moment, feeling an overwhelming urge to warn him about the consequences of breaking a pinkie promise. "Or you'll lose your pinkie."

A ghost of a smile tugs at his lips as he nods gently, mentally noting to not break the promise. *Because who would risk their pinkie.* Elias smirked after a moment before gently pressing his lips onto Aloura's slightly ajar ones.

"What was that for?" Aloura whispers as he pulls away.

Elias grinned, "My way of sealing a promise" Aloura laughed a little.

But I don't believe in promises.

Chapter Twenty

Aloura sighed at the sight of the house, cringing as her gaze fell onto the bloodied mess she'd left after this morning's beating. It seemed like whenever she'd get home from work, she'd find her *father* had drunkenly destroyed something. But Aloura paid no mind to the mess; instead making a beeline for the basement, in search of more information on who this organisation was. How her mother was involved.

And most importantly, Elias' connections to them.

Aloura made the cold floor a resting place, prying open the taped box and pulling out random sheets of paper- inspecting them for notes from her mother. She frowned at the lack of anything important. There was nothing much to see- mainly hospital notes from her workplace- and recipes she'd spent her life perfecting. Aloura sighed as she ran her hand through her locks, staring at the mess before her. She sighed again and began organising the papers into separate piles.

She lifted the sheets she'd already looked through and placed them in her mother's work pile behind her, before lifting more sheets of paper out of the box and into her lap. She frowned as she looked through them, her mother was a gynaecologist, and her farther a surgeon, why were there work sheets for an oncologist. Aloura flicked through the stapled sheets, dismissing the *patient confidentiality* stamped on the papers.

Details entailing the patient, who Aloura found to be, Katherine Kadar, and her chemotherapy treatments. Aloura's heart sank a little at the words written at the bottom; *deceased*. Aloura wasn't expecting to find much on the sheets of hospital information, but at the sight of underlined letters throughout the papers, Aloura grabbed a pen. Writing each letter underlined in a straight line, hopeful to make sense of her mother's clues.

Deliveringyoutoevilvictim174

Aloura's heart sank at the realisation, these weren't her patients, these people were the organisations victims.

She hastily placed the sheet to the side, and grabbed the next one; Edward Ren victim 86, except he didn't have cancer- but heart failure.

Aloura placed the sheet down and picked the next off her lap; June Stevens victim 91, brain Aneurism.

Aloura frowned at the common denominator being her father as their surgeon. *Is dad part of this organisation mama?* She thought to herself. *Were you?*

Aloura placed the sheets to her side, a reminder to take them with her to research. She lifted the next sheet of paper, a sinking feeling weighed her down as she stared at her own name in the sheets before her. Aloura Olea West.

Aloura breathed out as she pulled her eyes from the sheet. Too scared to read the remaining of the sheet. Her eyes fluttered shut for a moment and she swallowed the bile that rose into her throat before dropping her eyes back to the sheet.

Aloura Olea West: Michael West alms. Followed by a description of the young girl, signed off by her father. Aloura frowned. Her father was *offering* her.

Her mother had scribbled out the rest, writing a simple, but powerful, *no,* in the margins.

Aloura was angry, confused, the pit in her stomach seemed to be never ending- she'd swallow to fill it up, but it remained void. Aloura however, had no chance to grieve, her father's drunken footsteps echoed throughout the hallways. She froze and watched the stairs as his advancing figure neared her. She knew she had no time to hide the papers she'd looked through, so she made no attempt to cover up her actions. Instead, she rose up, her shoulders stiff as Michael stopped, his eyes fixated on the tipped-out boxes and the piles of paper spread throughout the basement floor.

Neither of them moved for a few seconds. They watched each other with angry eyes, although only one of them had the right to feel that way. "What is the meaning of this, girl?" he sneered after a moment, still not moving towards her. Aloura ignored him, an action she found herself surprised by.

"How did mama die?" Aloura questioned, her nose flared as she watched the shocked expression that filled her father's face.

He frowned, "don't talk to me like that girl. She got in an accident because of you" he pointed a grimy finger at her.

Aloura laughed bitterly, "was she protecting me from something" she lifted the sheet of paper to show him, although he was too far to be able to see what she was holding up anyway. "Because this paper has details on how I should be murdered."

Michael didn't reply, nor did his eyes meet Aloura's, they remained transfixed on the sheets of paper she held before her. This only angered the girl more, she took a daring step towards him, placing another sheet of paper in front of his face. "Who is delivering you too evil?" she took another step forward, "and what did they do to my mother?"

The mention of the organisation had clicked a switch in the drunk man's mind, his eyes had suddenly darkened, and his face scrunched up in anger. "Who the fuck do you think you are questioning me like this?" he stepped into Aloura's face, throwing a hit directly at her face.

His reaction was enough conformation to Aloura that whoever this organisation was, her father was a part of.

Elias sat at the edge of the rooftop, his eyes flickering to his watch every couple of seconds. Something he'd found himself doing a lot recently when it involved Aloura. His heart was basically in his mouth, and his stomach felt queasy. He knew why; it was two hours after he had agreed to meet. But he didn't know why he was felt anxious about her being late- maybe she had just fallen asleep or forgotten to meet up.

He sighed sadly and wiped the blood from the side of his lip for the hundredth time. He'd have to clean it himself if Aloura didn't show- but it felt wrong. *Aloura will be here*. He told himself. *She'll just apologise for being late and I'll have her clean me up.*

His eyes flew to the now cold box of cookies. He'd won the fight tonight and had gotten to baking her cookies the second he'd gotten home. Elias tore his eyes away from the container and into the sky, falling to the lone star Aloura had introduced him too.

"She's okay, right?" he asked the star. It didn't blink, Elias frowned, before sighing. "I'm going crazy."

He took a seat in their usual corner, resting his head on the cold wall, the rooftop felt cold without Aloura sat between his legs. It wasn't welcoming or comfortable like he'd felt it was when Aloura was reading to him and playing with his hair.

"I'll just sleep here, she'll come later or in the morning when she realises she slept in" Elias told the star, laughing lightly before closing his eyes.

The star didn't blink.

Chapter Twenty-One

Elias' head was pounding, and his neck felt cramped. He stirred in his sleep in annoyance at the light, he lifted his arms to pull his pillow onto his face, a shield from the blinding bulb. But he met the cold concrete. He paused for a split second, shutting his eyes tightly before prying one open and looking around.

His eyes shot open, and he pushed his body of the floor, his palms now flat onto the cold ground as he looked around the rooftop in confusion. He groaned as last night's events hit him, he was waiting for Aloura.

I was waiting for Aloura. He suddenly realised the weight of the situation, his hand shot to his phone, unlocking it and looking for any messages from the green-eyed brunette. "What the fuck?" he grumbled at the sight of no notifications. It was 10am, she had to be awake. He pressed her number and held his phone to his ear. "Pick up Aloura." He muttered to no one. "Pick up, please."

Elias pushed his body to stand as the phone rang, he paced around the rooftop, the phone pressed to his ear. A cold chill had settled down his spine, but he'd pushed it to be because of the cold metal held to his ear. That was soon proven wrong when Aloura's voice mail blared through the phone. Elias listened to her voice for a second before walking to the wall.

"Sorry I didn't pick up, I'm not available at the moment. I'll get back to you as soon as I can. Just leave a message after the beep!"

Elias ended the call as the beep rang into his ear. He paused for a moment his hands griping his phone anxiously before kicking the wall in front of him. "What the fuck Aloura." He kicked the wall again. "Where are you?"

His stepped back, and breathed in for a moment, his eyes shut in concentration. *Do I leave and look for you?* He asked no one in particular. *No what if you show up and I'm not here.* He answered himself.

He ran a hand through his hair as he unlocked his phone again, this time ringing Agnus. If anyone had seen her, it would have been her. Elias paced around again, adrenaline filling his body as he pictured unpleasant scenarios of Aloura hurt by the hands of Kaden- or worse yet, his boss.

No. no. I won last night.

Elias' train of thoughts were broken by Agnus concerned voice. "Elias dear? Are you there?"

Elias cursed in his head and stumbled on his words. "Yeah, yeah sorry" he muttered; his free hand flew to the back of his neck. "Sorry to bother you. I was just wondering if you've heard from Aloura?"

Elias could almost hear the older woman frown, before answering, "No dear. I'm afraid not. Is everything alright?"

Elias swallowed the lump is his throat and turned his head to the sky. Shutting his eyes in exhaustion. "No everything's alright" he lied between his teeth, "we were meant to meet but she didn't show."

"Oh, I'm sorry dear. I'm sure she's just running late." Agnus attempted to console him, but her words did nothing to put out the fire blaring in his heart. When Elias didn't reply, Agnus sighed. "I'll tell you what dear, I'll ring you as soon as she contacts me."

Elias smiled and nodded, before realising she couldn't see him. He swallowed and rushed out "Yeah. Yeah that would be great Agnus, thank you." He bid her farewell and ended the call, slipping his phone into his pocket. Elias sighed in defeat and took a seat into his previous resting place.

He pressed his head against the wall, and his hands down his face.

"Please be okay, I can't lose you before I have you."

♡ ♡ ♡

Aloura coughed into her locked fist, her shoulders shaking. She was tired, and in pain. Michael hadn't taken her questioning or snooping lightly. He'd inflicted the worst pain she'd felt upon her, and Aloura almost found herself wishing she'd stayed in her place.

He'd left her lying on the basement floor, bloodied and bruised. Not an inch of her wasn't aching. She had continuously tried to move to find her way into Elias' embrace at the rooftop, but her body was too heavy for her frail legs to carry. Or maybe it was her heart that felt too heavy. But either way, she lay there, where her father found her the next morning.

His heart clenched at his drunken actions; his hand tugged at his collar in guilt as he walked towards the passed out girl. Aloura's eyes flew open at the sound of his nearing footsteps, and when she'd saw his figure approaching her, she flinched up and coward away. Not mindful of her aching body.

"I'm sorry. I'm sorry" he called out with his hands up, "I'm just trying to help."

Aloura shook her head violently, as she pushed her sore body into the corner of the room. "Don't touch me" she begged, her voice laced with desperation and fear. "Please. It's fine. Please. don't touch me. I'm fine."

"Okay okay" Michael rushed out, tears now spilling from the brims of his eyes. "I'm not going to touch you. I won't touch you." He stared at the shaking girl for a moment before falling to his knees as he holding his head in his hands; spilling into a sobbing mess. "I'm sorry."

Aloura watched him with a broken heart, but she couldn't bring herself to feel sorry for him. Because what about her? What about her Mama? Did he not feel bad for them? She turned to face away, her chin resting on her bare shoulder as she swallowed the lump in her throat. She shut her eyes, a useless attempt to block out the sounds of her so called father's sobs. "how" he started after a few moments of crying. "How can I make this up to you?"

Aloura's lips trembled as she watched her desperate father plea before her. Aloura didn't need to think, there was only one thing in the world she ever wanted. "Bring back mama." *Or take me to her.*

Michael's teeth chattered angrily; he pressed his chapped lips together before standing up. "You're so fucking selfish." He yelled, grabbing her arm and pulling her to her feet. "I lost her too." He shook her, and she let him. Her clothes ripped and bloodied, her mind hazy. She had no fight left in her. "And every time I see you I see her." he punched the wall beside her head. "Every damn time."

"What did they do to her?" Aloura's voice came out strained and desperate. Michael's eyes flickered between hers. "What did you *let* them do to her?"

"It was your fault damnit." He cried, dropping the bruising grip he held Aloura with. "I didn't know she was going to *offer* herself."

Aloura's world stopped spinning. "Offer herself?"

Michael's eyes widened in realisation, he'd already said too much, and *they* have ears everywhere. In a quick motion, he grabbed Aloura's arm and dragged her up the staircase. Her screams of pain fell onto deaf ears as he dragged her to her room, grabbing a key from the basement hooks on the way up. "You already know too much." He snapped, pushing her into her empty room. "You think you've seen me angry? Step foot out this room and I'll show you how angry I can get." He slammed the door shut and locked it as she banged on the other side, begging and pleading to be let out.

Chapter Twenty Two

Elias' fist hit his head continuously lightly, his eyes felt heavy, but the weight of them seemed inconsiderable compared to the weight of his heart. Twenty four hours had passed without Aloura showing. Agnus had called a few hours before, apologising that the young girl had still not contacted her either.

Elias was cold, hungry and tired. He resisted the urge of just going home- *she probably just forgot. I'll see her at work tomorrow.* He attempted to convince himself. But he hadn't made it to the rooftop door before he shook his head. *Aloura had never left me hanging before. Plus, she still needs to clean my injuries.*

He called Blayde also, asking him to keep an eye out for the girl he'd saw in the photo the boss had given him, and asked Agnus to inform Cassidy too. *"Because I need to stay on the roof top for when she shows."*

"She's not gonna show man, go home. Its freezing out." Blayde had told him, but Elias scoffed back. She was going to show, and he was going to wait for her even if he had to wait his entire lifetime.

It was almost midnight when his phone rang, and Elias' eyes shot open, he rushed to grab his phone out his pocket, dropping it in the commotion. He cursed and grabbed it, paying no mind to the broken screen. "Aloura?" he rushed out, but the disappointment settled as Kalians giggles sounded through the phone.

"Is this a prank?" he giggled, "why would I be called Aloura?"

Elias swallowed the tight feeling that bundled up in his throat, forcing out a laugh at his little brother's words. "Hi buddy. How are you?" Elias didn't mean to feel disappointed upon hearing Kalian's voice, but the anxiety was eating him alive. He knew Kalian was well and safe, but the same couldn't be said for Aloura.

"Just missing you." Kalian's voice came out sad, he too didn't mean to burden his brother with the constant nagging and reminders of his short comings, but he missed his older brother. He had exhausted every birthday and Christmas wish on wishing to come home. Even making sure to add that he wanted to go home even if there was no home to go too. He just wanted his big brother.

"I miss you too buddy. How's school? Any girlfriends?" Elias smiled softly leaning his head onto the wall behind him. "Or boyfriends or enbyfriends?" he quickly added. Kalian laughed at this.

"No. how about you?" he giggled, wiggling his eyebrows although his older brother couldn't see him. "Specifically, someone called Aloura."

Elias laughed but didn't deny it which sent his little brother into a squealing mess, "Oh my god. Oh my god" he rushed out, Elias winced and pulled the phone from his ear. "Elias can I meet her? Please please please. I'm on my knees begging you right now. I'm telling you because you can't see me. Oh my god, Is she with you right now?"

"She's not with me right now" Elias laughed, "I was just waiting for her to call bud, and I can't get the call if you're on it."

Kalian gasped, "then why the heck did you pick up?"

"Watch your language little man" Elias frowned, before smiling as Kalian muttered out an apology. "Did you need anything?" he asked, although he knew what he had called to ask.

"uh" Kalian mumbled, pressing his face into his bed. "I just wanted to know how long until I can come." He whispered; his voice muffled by the bed sheets. But Elias already knew what he was asking.

"Soon buddy, I promise." Kalian resisted the urge to ask how soon, opting to stay on his brother's good side so he could meet the infamous *Aloura*. So, instead, he mumbled an okay, and wished his brother a goodnight, before reminding him how desperate he felt to talk to his girlfriend, then hanging up.

Elias held the phone to his ears even after the call ended, he pushed his legs to his chest, before resting his head on them. He didn't know why specifically he felt so defeated, but he'd never felt as lost and lonely as he did in that moment. His shoulders shook gently as sobs racked his body. He cried for his parents' death, for Kalian who was hours away with no family, for Aloura who had still yet to contact him, and for himself, who was forced to grow up before he had a chance to be young. He lifted his head and dropped it onto his knees a few times; in hopes of knocking this feeling, whatever it was, from his head.

"Please be okay" he cried into his knees. Except he didn't know if he was talking about Aloura, Kalian or himself. "Please."

♡ ♡ ♡

Elias didn't remember falling asleep, but he had woken up to the sound of the rooftop door banging and soft footsteps. He shot up and froze. He had hoped and willed for it to be Aloura but had not made reservations for what he would do when she came. His eyes scanned her, making sure she was really stood before him. "Aloura?" he whispered, more to himself than her, but she nodded anyway.
He stepped towards her, halting as he really took in her face and body.

She was even more bruised and bloodied than two days ago when she'd shown up to work late. Her clothes were torn and tattered, exposing random bits of her bruised and cut up body.

Elias swallowed his anger and stepped towards her cautiously. "Can I hug you?"

Aloura didn't reply, but she nodded, so Elias gently held her framed body as she relaxed into his embrace.

"It's okay sweetheart" he whispered to her, resting his chin on her head. "you're okay. I got you."

"What are you doing here?' Aloura sniffled after a moment, she gently pulled away and used her sleeve to wipe her nose and eyes.

"I was waiting for you."

"For two days?" Aloura's eyes widened as he nodded, "I'm so sorry I-"

"it's okay. As long as you're here now." Elias smiled at the shorter girl, his eyes once again fell on her bruises and his stomach tightened, and his jaw clenched. "Who the fuck hurt you Aloura?"

Aloura looked at his red eyes through her lashes, pushing down the anxiety that bubbled up inside her. "You're hurt too."

"Forget me Aloura, you're limping!" he growled, "I won't ask you again. Who the fuck did this to you?" when she didn't reply, he ran a hand through his hair. "No more secrets" he showed her his pinkie. "Remember?"

"Okay" Aloura swallowed. "No more secrets. You too?" Elias nodded, "Can we sit down?"

Elias nodded and held his hand out for her, she slipped hers into his, and they slowly walked to their usual corner; careful with Aloura's injuries. "Wait" he muttered as they reached their spot, he sat down before she could, and tapped his lap and watched Aloura who frowned at him. Upon seeing her apprehension, he sighed, "Aloura you're fucking hurt. I'll be dammed if I let you sit on the uncomfortable, cold floor."

Aloura could have sworn her heart jumped out her chest and ran a couple of laps around the rooftop by the speed it was beating. She smiled softly, and sat on his lap, her legs to the side of his body and her head resting on his shoulders.

"Please don't be mad" she started, Elias stared ahead of her and nodded gently, suddenly unsure if he wanted to actually know. "My dad uh, he's alcoholic and gets mad sometimes. He doesn't mean it I don't think, and he apologises most mornings. But yeah."

Elias glowered into the distance, the pounding of his heart claps of encouragement to beat the person who dared hurt his girl. "I'll fucking kill him."

"No. you can't. He's my dad." Aloura rushed out sitting up from his lap, wincing as she did so. Elias cursed, muttering an 'okay okay' to stop the girl from hurting herself more. He wasn't sure why she was protecting the person who had hurt her, but he didn't want to push her to hurt herself in his defence. So he gave in, silently imagining his hands around her father's throat instead. A few moments of silence passed between them before Elias spoke again.

"How long has this been going on?" His tone was sharp, Aloura shifted in his lap uncomfortably, she knew her answer would only enrage him more.

"Ever since my mum died. But somethings shady going on. I think he has something to do with her death." She muttered, without specifying the organisation, or the fact she'd seen the tattoo he had.

"Why do you think that?" he watched her as she played with the hem of his sleeve. She cursed in her mind, she didn't want him to ask, because now she was holding secrets. It was a good thing she didn't believe in promises.

"I found some stuff." Aloura looked up and met his gaze, "why're you always hurt?"

Elias wanted to press her for what she'd found. If it had anything to do with the people that were hurting him. He wanted to ask if anyone had approached her, but he didn't want to push her too far, so let the unspoken words out as a sigh instead. "My mum, she uh had cancer. The doctors caught it too late" Elias' throat felt like it was tightening around him as he spoke. "Her survival rate was so low, and my dad was desperate to save her." Aloura paused her playing with his sleeve, listening intently to his words. "So, when Dr. Lee approached my dad with this new treatment plan that cost more money that he'd ever even heard of, he jumped to the opportunity. This Dr knew people who could loan him the money. My dad didn't waste a second to sign it."

Aloura's heart fell, and the pieces had suddenly started to fit together.

"It was a scam" Elias laughed bitterly, "And my dad was stuck with the debt. They were shady people; he would have never been able to pay the money back. But that's what they wanted."

Aloura frowned at this. "What do you mean?"

"That's how they make money. By latching onto venerable people and making them spend the rest of their life paying more money than they even took."

"Did he manage to pay it back?" Aloura whispered, her heart heavy.

"He killed himself, and it was passed to me. That's why I'm always hurt. They make me box to win money to pay off the debt. But with every passing day, the debt increases." Elias scoffed, "in other words, I'm utterly and completely fucked."

Tears filled Aloura's eyes, "I'm sorry" she told him, he shook her off, muttering an 'it's not your fault.'

But it might as well have been, with Dr Lee being her so called father.

Chapter Twenty Three

Elias had noticed a shift in the girl's demeanour, she had become suddenly anxious, and he could practically see her mind spinning through her eyes. But he said nothing and leaned back and cradled her in his arms. Aloura had rested her head on his shoulder, her gaze fixated on the hem of Elias' sleeve. Elias' head rested on Aloura's as they watched the sky silently; too comfortable in the arms of the other to be the first to break the silence.

Aloura swallowed after a while, looking up to Elias with cautious eyes. "I'm scared" she confessed; her voice as timid as the look in her eyes.

Elias frowned, "what're you scared of baby?"

Aloura opened her mouth to speak but no words came out, she stared at Elias for a moment and breathed out. A futile attempt to calm the feelings that bubbled inside her. Elias' heart broke at the sight of the girls' quivering lips. He tightened his hold on her.

"Hey, hey. Please don't cry." He kissed her hair, "It kills me to see you like this."

Aloura's breath came out rugged, "He's going to kill me."

Elias scoffed at her words, frowning down at her. "Look at me Aloura" he told her when her eyes refused to meet his. She looked at him. "Do you really think I'm going to let that happen?"

Aloura sniffed and shrugged, too stubborn to admit she felt safe around him. Elias smiled a little, before answering his own question. "I'll set the world aflame before another hair of your head gets touched." He promised her. Aloura sniffed again and looked at him. He smiled at her gently. "I promise."

"I don't have anywhere to go-"

"If I have a place to go, then so do you." His voice firm but reassuring. "It's not much." He warned her, suddenly embarrassed he never bothered to decorate. But Aloura shrugged and smiled at him thankfully, anything was more than nothing.

The journey back to Elias' apartment was long and tiring, mainly because every movement sent a shot of pain through Aloura's body. Elias had offered to carry her, but that's where Aloura drew the line. She appreciated his efforts, but she didn't want to burden him. Afterall, he too was injured.

Aloura stood awkwardly as Elias' anxious hands pressed the key into the lock to open the door. His mind spinning with how messy he had left his house two days ago. He'd rushed to bake Aloura her cookies, and unable to contain his excitement to give them her, he left the dishes as a future him problem. He pushed open the door and motioned for Aloura to enter before him. "Uh" he messed his hair, "I'm sorry for the mess."

Aloura smiled at him gently, "I promise I don't mind. It could be a cardboard box and I'd still be thankful."

Elias' tense shoulders fell at Aloura's kind words, he offered her a small smile as they walked further into the apartment. Elias placed the keys on the side table as he slipped his shoes off. He watched Aloura as she scanned his home with curious eyes; lighting up at the picture of him and Kalian hung on the wall. "My brother" Elias called from behind her, Aloura turned to him, offering him an invitation with her eyes to tell her more. "He's called Kalian."

Aloura nodded and frowned at the realisation that he wasn't in the apartment, nor could he be with his parents unless he too had died. "Is he dead too?" Aloura's blunt words made them both wince. Her eyes widened as she quickly rushed out an apology. "I didn't mean it-"

Elias laughed, "it's okay. And no, he lives in Italy. It was too dangerous to keep him here."

Aloura frowned, "Why Italy?"

"My dad was half Italian" he explained, his eyes falling to the picture of his parents that hung on the wall.

"Woah" Aloura gasped. "So, you're basically Italian?" Elias' amused eyes fell to the gaping girl.

"Barely" he laughed, Aloura frowned at him.

"If I had any Italian in me I'd just tell everyone I was Italian." She grinned at him; his eyes twinkled at her smile.

"I have a couple inches of Italian I could put in you" he grinned at her cheekily.

Aloura's face flushed a crimson red. She swatted his chest, "eh, two inches? Would barely *feel* the difference."

Elias laughed at this, shaking his head at the suddenly cheeky girl. "You wound me Aloura." Aloura offered him a sarcastic pout. "Speaking of wounds. We should get you cleaned up."

Aloura frowned, "Only if I get to clean yours too." Elias watched her for a moment, she held his stare. He sighed and nodded. Aloura grinned.

 "The bathroom is too small" he laughed nervously, "so uh, I guess sit in the kitchen because we need a sink"

Aloura laughed, but didn't reply. She made her way to the kitchen, as Elias made his way to collect the first aid. Aloura placed her hands on the counter and lifted her body onto the countertop; kicking her legs aimlessly as she waited. Elias followed her after a few moments, a first aid kit in his hands. He placed the first aid kit beside Aloura, prying it open and taking out the antiseptic wipes, before turning to her.

Aloura parted her legs and made way for him to stand between them. Elias smirked at her but took the position with no complaints. She rolled her eyes at his childlike behaviour, but a small smile tugged at the corners of her lips. Elias placed the wipe on her cut, and she winced. He frowned, pausing his movements and rushing out a string of apologies. Aloura smiled up at him, her heart erratic as he placed a hand on her face; guiding it so he could tend to her wounds.

Elias' anger towards her father seemed to grow each second passing, and her soft winces and groans weren't doing much to ease the blaring fire in his heart. Aloura on the other hand, was getting bored of the silence that filled the kitchen. She grinned as Elias wiped the remaining blood from her eyebrow. Elias' eyes fell to her lip, furrowing his eyebrows together in question of what was so amusing.

Aloura's smile only widened as she lifted her legs and wrapped them around Elias' torso, teasing him. Elias swallowed as he watched their new positions, his eyes moving to stare at the innocent look Aloura shot in his direction. "My turn." She whispered, grabbing an anti-septic wipe and placing the tip of the package in her mouth, ripping it open.

Elias swallowed again; his eyes fixated on Aloura's every move. She moved slowly, pressing the wipe to the dry blood on his face, his gaze burning into her skin. Aloura readjusted her legs around Elias' pelvis, scooting her body further into his. Elias groaned at the contact, his hand flying instinctively to her hip, holding her in place. "Don't start what you won't finish, Aloura."

"Who says I wasn't going to finish it?" her voice low, daring.

Elias smirked, his hand remaining on her hip, and the other tucking a strand of hair behind her ear. He leaned down into her mouth, a taunting smirk plastered on his lips. "I said so sweetheart, because you're hurt right now." Aloura frowned at him, "but when I finally fuck you, I'll have you stumbling for weeks."

Aloura's face flushed red again, her mouth suddenly dry. "Come on" he grinned, stepping away, "I'll give you some clothes to change into."

He turned away to leave, before Aloura's voice called him over, he turned around as he neared the door. Aloura pointed to the first aid kit on the counter, "Uh, where do I place this."

He thought for a moment, "the shelf in the living room is fine"

Aloura nodded, before gathering the discarded items and placing them in the box. Elias had already left the kitchen when Aloura had finished gathering everything. She made her way into the living room, standing on the couch to reach the shelf. She steadied herself for a moment before peering on the shelf. Her eyes widening at the gun tucked behind the books. She watched it for a moment, her grip on the first aid kit tightening. She breathed out and placed the first aid kit where Elias had said before jumping off the couch. She shook the fear that filled her stomach.

Don't be fucking stupid she told herself, *he would never hurt me.*

Aloura caught her breath for a moment, before moving into Elias' bedroom. He stood at the wardrobe, gathering a change of clothes for both himself and Aloura. His head snapped to the door at the sound of Aloura's footsteps, smiling gently. "I don't think any of my bottoms will fit you" he told her, placing a large shirt and a pair of clean boxers in her hand.

Aloura watched as he handed her the clothes, before her eyes found him. "But um" she stumbled over her words, "my legs are." She started again, "they're filled with uh-"

Elias held her shoulders firmly, but his eyes held warmth and comfort that seemed to spill into Aloura, "I don't care about what's on or how your body looks like Aloura." He reassured her, "but I'll close my eyes as you get under the covers. Okay?" Aloura smiled and nodded.

Elias grabbed his change of clothes and walked to the bathroom. "Just get changed and get under the covers" he told her.

Aloura looked at the bed, and back at Elias' retreating figure. Had he not noticed the issue at hand? There was only one bed.

After a few moments of staring aimlessly at the door, Aloura slipped her tattered clothes off and slipped on the clothes' Elias had handed her. She stood before the body length mirror and admired the way Elias' clothes looked on her. Unsure if she should get into the bed or not, she remained standing awkwardly in the room, praying for Elias to come back.

Moments later, a closed eyed Elias walked through the door, his hands placed in front of him to guide himself through the room. Aloura giggled at the sight of him, and her heart swelled at how thoughtful he was. "You can open your eyes" she told him, "I don't mind anymore."

Elias' breath hitched in his throat as he opened his eyes, but he wasn't sure if it was because she trusted him enough to be vulnerable around him, or because of the sight of her in his clothes. "There's only one bed." She voiced her concerns.

Elias pried his eyes from her body and set them to her face. "I'm sleeping on the floor." He told her as he began to make the floor as comfortable as possible for himself. She frowned.

"Me too" she grinned at him after a moment, mirroring his actions of making a comfortable place for herself on the floor.

Elias frowned. "No, you're not. You're hurt."

"So are you" she scoffed, "plus, we slept together on the rooftop. So, we either sleep together in the bed, or on the floor." Aloura huffed, crossing her arms to show him how serious she was.

Elias rolled his eyes and a small smile tugged at his lips, "okay" he mumbled, placing his large hand at the small of Aloura's back, guiding her to the bed. Aloura's face burned red at his action. She lifted her body onto the bed, and Elias did the same, not commenting on how she slept on his side. "Goodnight Eli" Aloura mumbled, the last couple of days' exhaustions suddenly hitting her.

Elias' heart beat in his ears as he watched her eyes fluttered shut, he pulled her closer into his chest before kissing her hair. "Goodnight Aloura."

Chapter Twenty Four

Aloura's eyes flew open as the darkness faded away; sunlight now infiltrating the room. Her eyes scanned the room for a sign of Michael, a breath of relief leaving her lips at the reminder of what had commenced the day before. She attempted to snuggle herself deeper into the covers when she noticed the weight on her stomach.

She lifted the covers off her, grinning at the sight of Elias' arm gripping her waist protectively. She hadn't *ever* woken up snuggled in a bed before. Kaden's place had always long grown cold when she'd roll into it in the morning. Aloura grinned to herself, before lifting the white covers to her chin, and snuggling into Elias, who stirred in his sleep. "Good morning" she grinned at him as he opened one eye, cursing at the sunlight.

His scowl disappearing at Aloura's face, instead smiling softly at her, "good morning princess" Aloura's heart flipped at the nickname. She resisted the urge of kicking her feet around under the covers in excitement.

"What are we doing today?" she asked him, pushing her body into his, he wrapped his arms around her shoulders, kissing her forehead. He grinned against her hair at her use of *we* for talking about *their* day.

"We have work" he laughed at her pout, "and then I have training. I have a fight tomorrow." Aloura deepened her pout.

"Can I come?"

Elias scoffed, "to the fight? No way." He would rather have every finger plucked individually from his hands than agreeing to place Aloura in a scene so dangerous.

Aloura huffed, "But you said I was your lucky charm."

"You are" he promised her, "but it's too dangerous baby. How will I win if I lose you?"

Aloura rolled her eyes, "you know. It would be a shame if I tipped the police off about our age gap." she muttered, although it wasn't illegal, or that big of a gap.

Elias laughed at this, before swiftly pushing his body off the bed, encompassing Aloura beneath him. "You wouldn't."

Aloura frowned, how dare he underestimate the lengths she'd take? "sure I would" at the sound of her words, Elias' hands found Aloura's side before digging them in, sending the girl beneath him into a squealing mess.

"Take it back" he laughed, digging his fingers deeper into her sides, eliciting a string of pleas to stop; ones which he obviously ignored. "Take it back first."

"I take it back I take it back" Aloura squealed, gulping a large breath of air as Elias' hands retreated. "Can I at least come to your training?" Aloura plead.

Elias thought about it for a moment, before nodding, "I'll introduce you to Blayde" he told her. She grinned, and he matched it, before he dug his hands once again into her sides, sending the girl into another fit of giggles and squeals. "Okay seriously now" he laughed climbing off her, "we have to get ready, or we'll be late."

Aloura wheezed and nodded, she sat up on the bed, placing her hands protectively on her stomach in case Elias attempted to *viscously* attack her again. "You look so fucking beautiful in my clothes" Elias told her, Aloura looked down, suddenly aware she had no bottoms on.

"Stop looking or I'll seriously tell the cops" She warned, he laughed, before throwing a change of clothes and a new toothbrush in her face. "Kidding, kidding" she laughed, she seriously didn't want to be tickled again.

Elias threw her a fake scowl before walking out the door, offering her some privacy to change. He made his way to the kitchen, frowning at the empty cabinets. He sighed, and re heated last night's cookies, before grabbing two mugs and making them each a cup of coffee. Aloura made her presence as the microwave beeped. "I'm sorry I don't really have much to offer you" he mumbled, placing a plate of cookies and the mug where she sat.

"Are you kidding?" she frowned at him, grabbing his arm and turning him to her, "back at home I would have a glass of water at most." Elias frowned at this, although he had no right, because his routine wasn't much better. "Here I get a comfortable bed, a safe place, coffee and cookies!" Aloura rolled her eyes like it was obvious. "I'd consider myself the luckiest girl in the world."

Elias sighed out a breath of relief, her words providing him with much needed reassurance. "How did I get so lucky?' he kisses the tip of her nose.
Aloura blushes and spins to her food, ignoring Elias' words. He laughed, taking a seat beside her.

The pair of them ate in comfortable silence, occasionally catching the other staring, like each one of them couldn't believe to be in the presence of the other. When they'd finished, Elias moved to the bedroom to change, and Aloura rinsed out their dishes.

They walked hand in hand to the bakery, greeting Agnus and Cassidy with wide smiles. Agnus hadn't asked Aloura about her bruises, but deep down she knew. "Get ready, love birds" Cassidy laughed, throwing them an apron each. "This time, maybe stay out of the supplies closet" the pair blushed and caught their aprons, sauntering off to place them on. Cassidy laughed, she didn't really care, just loved teasing them.

Aloura's hands fumbled with the strings of her apron, she sighed and turned to find Annie; a ritual she had performed ever since she had started worked at the bakery. Her eyebrows furrowed when she couldn't locate Agnus.

Elias watched the lost looking girl in amusement, he probably should have intervened earlier, but it was too entertaining to pass the chance of seeing Aloura so helpless. "Need help?" he laughed as he made her way to her, tying his own apron with ease.

Aloura huffed at him, "No need to show off" Elias laughed and motioned for her to turn around. She hesitantly complied. Elias gruesomely moved in slow motion, attempting to prologue the girl's embarrassment for as long as he could.

"Eli" Aloura groaned. "I'm telling Agnus to fire you."

♡ ♡ ♡

Elias tightened his hold on Aloura's shaking hand as they reached the gymnasium door; a vain attempt to calm her nerves. Although he was anxious himself, not that he'd ever admit that out loud. He had never been given the chance to formally introduce *anyone* to his family or friends, so this was a large and important moment for him. And he desperately wanted to pause time and be able to experience it without the anxiety of *what if it goes wrong*.

"What if he punches my throat and tells me to fuck off?" Aloura asked, her face as serious as stone. Elias frowned down at the abnormal girl.

"Why the fuck would he do that?" Elias laughed, the worry suddenly at the back of his mind.

Aloura shrugged, "I don't know. You're the one who kept telling me he was a dangerous boxer called Blayde and if I was sure if I wanted to meet him" Aloura pulled a face. "You made him sound unhinged."

"Because he *is* dangerous" Elias laughed. "And he *is* called Blayde" His laughter running short as someone scoffed behind them. The pair turned to face an offended looking Blayde.

"Don't listen to him sweetheart" he grinned at Aloura, before shooting Elias a disapproved glare. "I'm anything but dangerous." Elias sneered at Blayde, for both the nickname and the lie. "I'm Blayde" he held out his hand.

Aloura shyly placed hers in his, "Aloura." Blayde nodded, and shook her smaller hand, before lifting it and placing a gentle kiss on her knuckles. Elias frowned, grabbing Aloura from his grasp and tucking her into his side.

"Not my girl, dickhead" he snapped, although humour was evident in his voice. Aloura thanked the skies that Elias had a firm hold on her, because her knees would have buckled beneath her at the sound of his words.

"Elias jealous? I would have never even dreamed of this day" Blayde laughed out loud. "Come on now pretty boy" Blayde tapped Elias' shoulder. "We have a lot of work to do." He told him, before turning to Aloura. "Sorry sweetheart, I'm stealing your boyfriend for a while."

Neither Aloura nor Elias corrected him.

Chapter Twenty Five

Pay day might as well be a national holiday, because Aloura couldn't ever remember ever being this excited for Christmas, or thanksgiving. She had continuously checked her bank to make sure she really had *all* that money for herself; now that she did not need to spend it all on her father's addictions. Elias hadn't worked at the bakery long enough to make enough cash, so after Aloura's constant nagging, the pair agreed to go grocery shopping. With Aloura's paycheque of course, it was the least she could to do thank him for taking her in.

"No, I want to push it" Aloura moaned as Elias beat her to the trolly stand, inserting a coin and pulling the trolly from its place.

Elias *maturely* laughed in her face, "well too bad isn't it?" he grinned back at her, purposefully pushing it faster than needed, making her run to catch up. "Should've gotten to it before me."

Aloura frowned at him, "it's not my fault your legs are like twenty meters long!"

Elias scoffed, halting the trolly at the sound of her insulting words, "they are not" he told her. "Yours are just in the minus'. That's not my fault."

Aloura huffed as she caught up with them, holding onto the trolly to annoy Elias. If she couldn't have the trolly, then he couldn't enjoy having it. "That's not even possible"

"Sure it is. Look at you, defying all the odds" he laughed, wiggling the trolly side to side in a futile attempt of getting Aloura's grip off it. "Let go. you're making it heavier to push."

"Good" Aloura grinned as they neared the supermarket entrance, Elias groaned but let her keep her hand on the trolly, "what do we need?" Elias thought for a moment and shrugged, Aloura narrowed her eyes at him.

"We can just go down the aisles until we see something we need?" Elias suggested after a moment, Aloura grinned and nodded, guiding the trolly to the first aisle. Grocery shopping was exciting, especially when she knew her cart wouldn't be filled with different alcohols. "Are you allergic to anything?" Elias asked after a moment of walking in silence.

Aloura tore her gaze from the different cereals that sat lined up perfectly, settling it on Elias' inquisitive face. "No. I wish. Are you?" Elias shot her a weird look.

"No, and why do you want to be allergic to something?" Aloura shrugged, turning her gaze back to the cereal boxes.

"Just sounds cool" Elias laughed at this, "I'd just be like hi I'm Aloura and I'm allergic to peanuts."

"Why would you mention your allergy when you introduce yourself?" he laughed at her as she grabbed a box of crunchy nut cornflakes, placing it in the cart. Aloura shrugged again. Elias shook his head and pushed the trolly further down the aisle. Aloura placed her hand back on the trolly, shaking it as they walked. Elias frowned at her. "Stop that"

"Stop what?" she grinned innocently.

Elias scoffed, muttering a "you know what" Aloura shrugged in response, feigning confusion. "I'm gonna make you sorry for this" he warned her, blissfully unaware of how *sexually wrong* Aloura took it.

Aloura grinned at the sight of the empty aisle, stepping in Elias' face, "and how are you going to do that?" she smirked, her voice seductive.

Elias swallowed; his eyes wide as he watched Aloura's advances. She stood on her tiptoes, checking the aisle one more time before guiding her hand dangerously close to Elias' crotch; but not touching him. Elias' face lowered down to hers, their eyes engrossed on each other's lips.

Elias' breath was practically fanning Aloura's lips when she broke out in a grin, before swerving his advances and grabbing a hold of the trolly, pushing it down and giggling in victory. A stunned Elias watched the triumphed girl practically skipping with glee. "Hey!" he called after her, "I wanted to push it. I had it first"

Aloura grinned back at him, "Too bad isn't it?" she shot his words back at him, "don't think with you dick next time."

♡ ♡ ♡

It was almost ten at night when the pair had arrived home, shopping bags in hand. Aloura had, in fact, managed to keep the trolly the entire shopping trip. Although they both knew Elias had let her keep it, not that either of them would admit to that.

Elias had instructed Aloura to change into more comfortable clothes while he put the shopping away, and Aloura complied, making her way to the bedroom. She picked up the clothes from the night before, slipping them on before walking to his nightstand.

She didn't mean to snoop, she had originally only wanted to place the clothes into the washing basket but at the sight of familiar documents on his nightstand, she couldn't resist the urge. Aloura frowned and picked them up, her heart sinking at the realisation of where she'd seen these documents before.

Hospital documents, for Katherine Kader.

"Hey, I was calling for you, are you okay?" Elias asked, his head popping through the door. Aloura flinched at the sudden sound and turned to face Elias, sheets still at hand.

"Yeah sorry, I just found these uh" she spoke awkwardly, placing them back where she'd found them, "your mother is um, Katherine Kader?" she asked him.

Elias nodded, confused at her sudden shift in demeanour and sudden interest. "Yeah. You okay?" Aloura nodded and swallowed. "Are you sure?" his voice worried. Aloura took a moment to clear her mind, before nodding again. "Okay come on then" he grinned at her, "I heated up some food for us."

Aloura smiled at his words, suddenly forgetting the dilemma she had found herself in. she couldn't remember the last time she had a hot meal that wasn't Annie's work lunch.

Aloura followed Elias to the living room, where he had placed two bowls of pasta and a can of diet coke each. Aloura smiled at him as she took a seat, thanking him for the food. "Don't thank me, you're the one who bought it." He told her sincerely. "I should be the one thanking you"

Aloura placed a forkful of pasta in the entrance of his mouth, Elias parted his lips and took the bite, watching Aloura with soft eyes. "It was nothing" she told him. *I'd die for you if I had too.*

Aloura watched Elias' lips as he chewed, he turned to look at her, his own pasta on a fork at the entrance of her mouth. It was now her turn to part her lips and bite down. The moment more sensual than the pair had intended.

Elias watched Aloura, and Aloura watched Elias. Both swallowing the food and pausing to admire each other. Their faces moving inches apart now, and eyes softly shut. Aloura moved to meet Elias' lips, lifting her body slightly off the coach.

Aloura's stomach churned with excitement at the feeling of Elias' soft lips against hers. His lips movement synchronic with her own, his tongue grazing her bottom lip, pushing it into her mouth. Aloura didn't part her lips for him, making Elias frown into the kiss. He pushed his tongue again, and Aloura giggled into the kiss, still not giving way. Elias' teeth pulled at Aloura's bottom lip for a moment, seizing a moment for them to catch their breath.

Lips still locked, he hastily moved the dishes from their hold, and with his now empty hands, he pushed Aloura back, leaning into her. She gasped as her back met the cushion of the couch, and Elias smirked into her mouth, pushing his tongue into her now open mouth. Their tongues tussled into each other, tangled in Aloura's mouth.

Aloura lifted her hand, placing it on Elias' cheek, evoking a groan from the boy. He repositioned them, grabbing the breathless girl from the back of her thighs, and carrying her into the bedroom, their lips remaining locked.

He carefully placed her body onto the bed, before positioning a knee on each side of Aloura's body. He broke away, their ragged breathing filling the room. He leaned into Aloura, attaching his lips to the curve of her exposed neck. Aloura lifted her head, giving Elias' mouth access to her body. Sounds of pleasure spilling from her lips and into Elias' ears; cries of encouragement to keep going.

Elias' hands found Aloura's waist, the pair shivering at the skin contact where Aloura's shirt had risen. She moved her face towards his, and he once again their lips connecting. Aloura's hands ran down Elias' chest, grabbing the hem of his shirt and pulling it up gently. Elias lifted his arms as she slipped the shirt off him, an act of silent consent.

His body was tanned and defined, with random bruises littering it. Her hands caressed through the knots in Elias' shoulders, before trailing to his biceps. Elias moaned into Aloura's mouth; the sound dampening the meeting of her thighs. He pulled away from

Aloura, grabbing the hem of her shirt, his eyes meeting hers. "Is this okay?" he mumbled as he kissed her jaw. Aloura nodded, "you gotta tell me with your words sweetheart" Aloura's heart fluttered.

"Yes" she mumbled out, "it's okay."

Elias watched her for a second, making sure she meant the words she said before nodding. He pulled the shirt over her head. He swallowed at the sight of her under him, in nothing but his boxers and a red bra. He kissed her shoulder blade, and she ran her hand through his hair, wrapping her legs around his torso.

Elias sucked at her skin, leaving trails of love bites on her. The juxtaposition of the mix of bruises and love bites on her skin was almost poetic, ironic even. His lips trailed down her body, his hands following suit, finding the clasp of her bra. He looks at her and she nods before he has the chance to ask, desperation filling her eyes. Elias' fingers unclasp her effortlessly, guiding the straps softly off her shoulders before discarding it on the floor.

 His eyes follow her brazenly exposed breasts that seemed to be made to fit in his hands. He rolls her erect pink nipple between the tips of his fingers. Aloura moaned in response, her hands running down Elias' back, and legs tightening around his body, before letting go.

 Elias leans down to her chest, capturing a nipple in-between his lips, his tongue flicking it as he does so. He lifted his knee slowly, pressing it between her thighs, gently adding pressure to her now swollen clit. Aloura's hips lifted off the bed in response, the wetness now hard to miss, as she desperately pushed her body into the centre of pleasure. Elias' lips dropped her nipple, his hand grasping her hip and pushing her back into the bed harshly, but not enough to hurt her. "You get what I give you, and nothing more." He tells her, his breath fanned her ear as he whispered, "don't move your hips off the bed." His voice so commanding Aloura found herself nodding before she could stop herself, her better judgment hazed by pleasure.

Elias smirked at her submission, pecking her lips as he pressed more pressure onto the bundle of nerves between her thighs. Aloura raggedly inhaled, an impotent attempt to calm her body's reaction to Elias' touch. He kissed her jaw again, and her hands found their way to his sweatpants, kneading his bulge through the material. She looked up at him, only to see him already watching her with hungry eyes. He nodded to her gently, using his own hands over her smaller ones to guide her in pulling his sweatpants off.

Aloura swallowed, and looked into his eyes, her hands making their way over the material as he pressed small kisses on her collar bone. Aloura's hand movements were swift and tight around his shaft, and Elias found himself holding his breath and prepping kisses a few seconds longer than he'd intended. He swallowed and moved his lips lower down Aloura's body, lingering at the hem of her underwear, before biting her gently. He pulled at her underwear with his teeth and watched Aloura squirm as the elastic fell back on her silky skin, smirking. He looked at Aloura, once again, asking with his eyes for permission.

Aloura ran her hands through his hair and nodded once again, he holds her gaze as he pulls them off, discarding them on the floor. Aloura frowns at him, "what're you waiting for?" she whispers, but he doesn't move, his eyes remain on hers, as if asking for permission to see the rest of her. And when she doesn't shy away, his gaze lowers. His eyes trace over every curve of her body, her every imperfection and insecurity hanging out on display for his eyes. Like an art exhibit, her body the main attraction.
And boy was he attracted.

And in that moment, as he looked from Aloura's face to what sat at the meeting of her thighs, he knew where all the goodness and beauty in this world was. It was no wonder the world was bleak, whoever was above had given it all to the woman that lay beneath him. "Eli?" her timid voice broke him from his trance, his silence had made her grow anxious. Her hands now wrapped pathetically around her; her legs pressed shut.

Elias frowned, he moved up swiftly, grabbing her hands and pinning them above her head, "don't hide yourself from me" he whispered, pecking her lips. "You look *so* beautiful."

Chapter Twenty Six

Aloura watched Elias through the valley of her breasts, and between her legs. Her gaze burning into his skin, he looked up at her. He moved over to her face, pressing his middle and ring figures into her mouth. She parted her lips and latched onto them, her eyes holding his through her lashes. Elias groaned at the sight of her. Aloura swirled her tongue on his fingers salvaging on them, before he pulled them out. He pecked her lips and moving back to his place between her parted thighs. "Is this okay?" he asked her, she nodded in response.

Elias nodded and swallowed, pressing his lips around her clit, and his now moist fingers at her entrance. He pushed his fingers gently, pausing as Aloura tensed around him, her hands tangled in his hair. He gave her a moment to readjust with his fingers in her, before pushing the remainder into her, curving his fingers as he retracted and pressed them back in. Aloura's body stiffened, her hands pulled at his hair, and her head now thrown backwards, her body in blissful pleasure.

Elias' tongue swirled and pressed her clit, and Aloura couldn't help the moans that spilled out her mouth. The room now filled with Aloura's wet scent, and Elias could have sworn he was high on it. He sped his fingers inside her, curling them once more and repetitively hitting the spot inside her. Aloura pulled in a lungful of air, her hips suddenly hovering off the bed.

Elias' movements halted, his fingers remained in the girl as he moved the other hand and laid it flat on the girl's stomach, pushing her body down. "What did I say, Aloura?" he asks her, his voice daring. Aloura swallows, she opens her mouth to speak, but Elias' fingers curl inside her again, "hmm?" he asks, the heel of his palm hitting her clit, his movements now faster.

"Don't move my hips off the bed" she moans out, her voice broken and coated in pleasure. Elias nods, his fingers speeding inside her, hitting her g spot retentively. Aloura closes her eyes in pleasure.

Elias clicks his tongue and speeds his fingers inside her once more. "Open your eyes Aloura, I want you to look at me as you cum."

Aloura squeezes her eyes tightly shut before pushing them open, locking them with Elias' who watched her intensely, her thighs tightening around his hand. Elias watched the girl beneath him dissolve into pleasure, trails of fire growing in the pits of Aloura's stomach as she rode his fingers.

Aloura shuddered uncontrollably as sensation of blinding reales filled her core. Elias pressed his lips on hers as she came down from her climax, pulling his fingers from the shaking girl, he pulled down his boxers and used them as lubrication for his own pleasure.

He reached to the nightstand, and pulled a condom out, he looked at Aloura and held it up for her to see, "can I fuck you?" he asks. Aloura's eyes widen at his blazon language, when she doesn't reply, Elias pulls her ear lobe into his mouth, biting gently, "can I fuck you?" he asks again.

Aloura nods, before whispering out a "yes" after realising he'd asked for verbal consent.

Elias once again, watches her for a moment to make sure she was certain. He nods after confirming with himself and placing the corner of the condom package in his mouth, ripping it open, his eyes fall to Aloura's parted thighs, his arousal growing at the sight of her swollen clit.

Elias placed a few strokes on his dick, his eyes latched to Aloura's body, his pace speeding. "you're so fucking mesmerising Aloura" he told her, "So fucking mesmerising."

Aloura blushed at his words, her wetness deepening at the sight of him pleasuring himself over her. "Are you ready baby?" he asked her as he positioned his girth at the slit of her entrance. After she nodded, Elias held his dick her entrance before moving it along the slit of her entrance. Gathering all her wetness and spreading it towards her clit before pressing pressure on her bundle of nerves, eliciting a moan from the aroused girl.

"Eli" she moaned; her eyes sealed shut as she anticipated his thrust that he seemed to never want to give her.

Elias grinned at the sight of the needy girl, "yes baby?" she moans in reply, and he chuckles at this. "You gotta tell me what you want doll." He moves his hand to her sex and rolls her clit in his fingers whilst jerking himself off.

Aloura moans through the pleasure, she swallows and forces her words out. "Elias. *Fuck me. Please fuck me.*"

Elias groans at her words, His right hand remained on her clit as he grabbed her left hip, guiding his dick into her entrance before thrusting into her. Aloura's mouth flies open at the stretch of him, but no sounds left it. Elias paused after a moment, giving the squirming girl time to relax her muscles around him.

Aloura moaned, and looked up at Elias, who awaited her consent to move again, he smirked at her, before pulling out and slamming himself back into her, *"can you feel the Italian now baby?"*

♡ ♡ ♡

Aloura eyes flew open in a hurry, her eyes once again scanning the room around her, her shoulder falling back as she realised she was safe. She turned her head up, before smiling at Elias' sleeping figure; he looked so peaceful.

The both were still clothe-less, with Aloura's body pressed against Elias' his arms cradling her protectively. Aloura's face flushed at their position, she pried Elias' arms off her body, careful not to wake him. Once successful, she grabbed a fresh change of clothes, and turned away from Elias, changing into them.

"I could get used to this view" Elias' voice hoarse as he mumbled from the bed after she'd finished getting changed. Aloura flinched and turned around with wide eyes. Elias had sat up in the bed, his upper body bare. He had prepped his hands at the back of his head, making his biceps bulge, as he watched Aloura.

Aloura flushed a deep shade of red, suddenly wishing the earth would swallow her. Elias grinned at her, before throwing the covers off him, not caring for *his junk* that stood on show. Aloura shrieked and covered her eyes with her hands. Elias frowned and stood in front of her prying her hands from her face. "You were literally riding it last night" he laughed.

Aloura blushed again, keeping her eyes secured on high grounds around the apartment. "That's different!"

Elias laughed and grabbed his discarded boxers off the floor before slipping them on, putting the suddenly shy girl out of her misery. "Happy now?" he laughed.

Aloura's eyes dropped to his now covered body and nodded, "much better"

Elias laughed at this, he wrapped his arms around Aloura's shoulders, encompassing her in a hug. Aloura melted in his warm embrace as he gently rocked them. "You okay?" he asked after a moment. Aloura nodded and looked up at him, shooting his own question back at him. To which he nodded. Smoothing out her brown locks before planting a kiss on her forehead. "I have a fight tonight"

Aloura's shoulders tensed in worry, she gulped and stepped away from him. He frowned at her, "Do you want to come with me for the training?"

Aloura shook her head, she had her own plans; ones she didn't intend on sharing with Elias. "I'm going to the library." She put it simply, missing out crucial information that would have warranted disapproval from Elias.

Elias smiled and nodded, he grabbed a change of clothes and walked to the bathroom, leaving a guilt filled Aloura behind. She ran a hand through her hair in frustration. *Don't feel guilty* she consoled herself, *I'm just trying to help*. Aloura found solace in her own words, suddenly feeling less iniquitous.

After she had made sure Elias was no longer re-entering room, she walked to the previous papers she'd found at his nightstand, snapping a photo of them, before tucking her phone in her pocket. She knew what she was doing was wrong, but she had to find what her father's connection to this organisation was, and most importantly if he was the Dr. Lee Elias had told her about.

Aloura gabbed the small number of belongings she had, searching their pockets for her mother's old notes; hoping she hadn't left them behind in her hurry of getting out her house. She sighed in relief after she'd found them in a pile under her bag. She grabbed them and placed them into her bag. She would need these later. Elias' figure appeared a few moments later, "do you want toast?" he asked her, placing his freshly filled water bottle in the bag and handing her a mug of coffee.

Aloura shook her head, taking a sip of the hot liquid, "I'm not hungry, thank you."

♡ ♡ ♡

Aloura frowned at the keyboard, her mind was foggy, and she felt lost- where does she even start? Aloura had spread her mother's notes messily around the desk, unsure on what piece of information she was meant to look at first.

She grabbed a piece of plain paper, and a pen she'd found in Elias' living room, before titling the page, 'things I know.' And with that, she began to list every fact she had come to find out since her initial finding of the organisation. She listed how her mother's death was some sort of offering, connected to the gang. How Elias' mother was Katherine Kader, the gangs one hundred and seventy fourth victim, and a patient of her fathers. She noted how her father, Dr Lee had approached Elias' dad.

After she sat back, she frowned, everything on the paper seemed connected, but the bigger idea seemed to be missing. She turned to the laptop, typing in her mother's name. She guided the mouse to the first link and sat back as it loaded, her mouth suddenly dry.

Car Accident on the M1 reported to not be accidental Chief of police says.

Aloura looked away from the screen, tapping her fist slightly on her knee as an encouragement to read on. She gave herself a few moments to gather herself together before looking back to the documents.

Eyewitnesses reported two matching vans, with words that are yet to be released public, chasing a car down. "It looked like they were both targeting this one car" one eyewitness told reporters. "Police are treating this incident as a homicide investigation."

Lastly, a picture of her mother's car wrecked, with the caption: *No survivors.*
Aloura frowned, unsure on how any of this was related to the offering her father had told her about.

Aloura noted down some information on the article on the piece of paper, circling the contact numbers she'd stumbled upon, before leaving the article. Now searching for Elias' mother. She sighed in annoyance as nothing except Facebook posts concerning her death appeared. Aloura sat back in her chair, the tip of the pen in between her lips as she stared at her notes.

She took the pen out her mouth and wrote his mother's name, circling it and writing "Dr Lee" with question marks all over. Aloura suddenly sat up and searched "Doctor Michael Lee." Aloura tapped the table with her pen as her searches loaded up.

As the screen finally started loaded up, Aloura felt her vision become blurred, and her eyes began to ring. She dropped her pen and gripped the edge of the desk to steady herself.

Michael Lee medical licence evoked after connections with Dute.

"Dute" Aloura whispered, "delivering you too evil."

Chapter Twenty Seven

Aloura sat frigid at the kitchen counter in Elias' apartment. Her mind felt foggy, a feeling she'd found herself familiar with. She stared out into the wall, unsure on how handle emotions this big. Unsure on how to handle any emotions actually, specifically ones this big.

It was days like this she missed her mother the most, she craved for a lap to crawl into, for her mother's hand to play with her hair. She could almost imagine how comforting it used to feel.

"Why couldn't you just leave me a letter or something so I could understand everything at once ma?" Aloura scoffed to the empty seat beside her. Aloura frowned at her own words, "Who did you talk to this about- Annie. Oh my god, why didn't I think of that." She muttered to herself, although it was her who had thought of it.

Aloura reached for her bag, grabbing the sheets of paper she had filled in earlier, "I hope for my sanity you know something

Annie" Aloura mumbled. "I need a plan of action."

She turned the sheet over, writing 'plan of action' at the top before sitting back. "Whoever gets my notes if I die trying to figure this out is one lucky son of a bitch." She laughed awkwardly, desperately trying to find humour in the situation. "Because unlike someone" Aloura mumbled, shooting a funny look to the ceiling, "I'm not writing in riddles and morse codes."

Aloura scribbled down the steps onto her plan paper.

Step One: Talk to Annie
Step Two: Talk to Michael
Step Three: figure out step three

Aloura didn't really know what she was looking for, but a journey with no direction would still lead somewhere.

♡ ♡ ♡

Aloura's knee shook as she sat in gruesome silence, Elias was late, and Aloura was anticipating how injured he was this time. Especially considering the fact she now knew how dangerous these people were. Aloura leaned her head in her hands and counted to sixty again in her head- an attempt to calculate how late he was, while also passing time.

Aloura's body shot up from the couch at the sound of the keys turning in the door, she practically ran to meet Elias, forcing herself to not throw her arms around him in case he was seriously injured. "Hi baby" he grinned at her, wincing at the sudden movements. Aloura frowned at his injuries.

"You're hurt" she told him like he couldn't feel it. Elias laughed, but Aloura's expression stayed stone cold. *We say that phrase a lot* she thought as she walked towards Elias, *maybe it's our okay.* Aloura steadied Elias' frame and helped him walk through the apartment.

"You should've seen the other guy." He grinned as they made their way to the kitchen- their newly agreed surgical bed. "Would you feel better if I told you I won? The lights will be up the entire month this time." He grinned, Aloura's heart sank at his words- she was happy for him, but no one should have to go through all this just for lights in their house.

 "it's going to be like the north pole in this house." She smiled softly at him, deciding she'd rather not dampen his mood with her anxious thoughts. She turned and grabbed the first aid kit she'd set up before his arrival, prying it open.

Elias frowned at her words, "the north pole?" Aloura nodded at him slowly. "Are you cold?"

"No, because of the northern lights." She told him like it was obvious.

"Why would you use that analogy?" Elias laughed at her, "when I said lights stay on, I didn't mean disco lights." Aloura pressed on his wound with the wipe making him wince, "sorry, sorry."

Aloura stood in between Elias' parted legs, holding his jaw gently, wiping away the remainder of the blood on his face; cringing every time Elias flinched. Aloura used her hand to guide Elias' face around, blushing at the sight of the hickeys on his neck. "I hate to see you like this" she told him sadly.

Elias swallowed, "I hate for you to see me like this too baby, I'm sorry." He had never meant to drag her into this lifestyle, she didn't deserve this burden- this was his baggage to carry.

"Is it going to be like this forever?" she asked him gently, throwing the used wipe and picking up a new one. Elias watched her mouth as she tore it open with her teeth before answering.

"I hope not"

Aloura nodded, "how much do you owe?" Elias flinched, he knew this question was coming, but he hadn't expected it so soon in their relationship, or whatever what they had was.

Elias considered lying for a moment, the subtotal was a large amount, and he was fearful Aloura would realise this is how life would be forever. *No more secrets* he reminded himself, stealing a glance at his pinkie, *I don't want to lose my pinkie*. "Sixty four thousand"

Aloura's movements froze, she looked at him with a gaping mouth and wide eyes but said nothing. Elias' knee bounced in anxiety, praying on every wishing well and every shooting star that his words hadn't deterred the green eyed beauty.

Aloura didn't comment, and Elias was unsure if that was a good sign or not, but he settled in the silence for a moment, before breaking it. "How was the library?" Elias mumbled.

Aloura stiffened at the memory of the information she'd obtained today, she swallowed the words she desperately wanted to tell him, settling for half-truths instead. "It was okay."

Elias frowned at her vagueness, "did I do something?" he asked her softly, ready to apologies for whatever fuck up he'd unknowingly caused. But Aloura didn't hear him, her ears ringing from the fogginess of her brain. Elias' Sixty four thousand debts replaying in her mind. Elias gently placed his hands on her cheeks, forcing her out her trance. "What did I do baby?" his voice laced with sadness, his guilty eyes flickering between hers.

"What? Nothing, what do you mean?" Aloura frowned. Elias sighed in relief, but his heart remained heavy; even if it wasn't him she was upset with, the mere fact she was upset was enough to ruin his day. Elias held her wrist gently, prying the antiseptic wipe from her grasp. Intertwining their hands together, he slid off the counter and walked her to the living room.

He gently pushed her into the cushion of the couch, "talk to me," he took a seat beside her, "what's on your mind?"

Aloura thought for a moment, "I want to see my dad." She had only said that fearing her heart would spill the words her mind desperately wanted to keep private.

Elias shot her a look of disconcert; perplexed by her sudden interest in talking to her father. "Over my dead body, Aloura" he spoke, his tone final, "He'll kill you. You said it yourself last time!"

Aloura frowned at him, confused as to where she'd asked. "Elias I wasn't asking you. I was telling you." Aloura spoke slow, her eyes dark and Elias almost flinched at them.

"I said no Aloura." Elias snapped, growing impatient. He didn't mean to be so controlling, but he couldn't help but feel scared for the girl. The last time she was with him, he beat her until she could barely walk, before locking her in her room. He was only trying to protect her.

Aloura frowned at him, "you're exactly like Kaden" she told him, although she didn't mean it. Elias' anger only grew. "So fucking controlling."

"I'll start cheating, then you can actually mean it when you say it."

Chapter Twenty Eight

Aloura couldn't remember how exactly she had found herself in Elias' bed, because she remembered sleeping on the couch the night before. She knew the only explanation was that Elias had moved her here after she'd fallen asleep and taken the couch for himself. Aloura's heart fluttered at his gentleman nature, even when they were angry at each other.

Aloura threw the covers off her body, sitting upright on the bed, before tucking her knees to her chest. She rested her back on the headboard, and her head on her knees. She wasn't necessarily upset at Elias; she too had said hurtful things, but she was unsure how she was going to apologies when she meant most of the things she said.

She really did need to talk to her dad, *this was his mess after all*.

She wanted Elias out of this debt now, no matter what it cost. And the more she thought about it, the more she'd realised how little sixty four thousand was to what she was willing to lose for him to have a normal life.

Aloura's alarm rang, and her heart fluttered in her chest once more. Elias had set her phone alarm so she wasn't late for work. *Fuck you* she mentally cursed him, *why're you so easy to love. I want to be mad at you.*

Aloura reached over to the nightstand and unplugged her phone, before turning the alarm off and throwing it onto the bed. she groaned and threw her body onto the bed also, giving herself a few moments to collect her emotions before getting ready for a day filled with fake smiles and white lies.

Aloura slid off the bed, and grabbed her change of clothes from the pile, and slipped them on. She grabbed a hair tie from the nightstand and threw her hair into a ponytail.

Elias was nowhere in the flat when she had wondered into the kitchen. She could practically hear her heart breaking slightly at the thought of him still mad at her. She stood aimlessly in the centre of the kitchen; eyes fixed on the first aid kit neither of them had bothered packing away. She swallowed the lump in her throat, suddenly losing appetite.

Instead, making her way to the bakery, hopeful Elias had just decided to turn up to work early, and not seriously injured somewhere from last night. She paused outside the door, gathering her thoughts before pushing it open. She pulled her best smile onto her lips and greeted Cassidy, before walking off to the back of the bakery. She pulled open her locker, pushing in her belongings, and taking out her work apron.

Aloura rushed out the back whilst slipping the apron through her head, her eyes scanning the diner floor for Elias' familiar figure, disappointment settling in the pits of her stomach as she realised he wasn't there.

Her hands fumbled with the strings of her apron, groaning in frustration. She all but tied them when two larger hands covered hers, guiding her fingers to aid her in tying the apron up. Aloura didn't need to turn around to know it was Elias that was behind her, because only his touch made her body this hot and flustered. "You just gotta loop both strings" he told her as he looped the strings. "Then wrap the loops together." Aloura blinked before nodding. "Try do mine." He told her, turning around.

Aloura smiled softly, grateful he wasn't one to hold a grudge. Aloura held the two ends of the string in concentration, her teeth clamped on her tongue that rested out her mouth. Aloura followed the instructions Elias had relayed to her mere seconds ago, before stepping back. Smiling in victory. "Oh my god I did it!" Aloura grinned up. Elias laughed at her.

"You did it." Elias smiled fondly at her, "I'll always tie your apron and you gotta always tie mine" he told her, Aloura grinned, nodding her head. "It's a deal then, sweetheart"

"Elias I'm sorry about what I said-" Aloura mumbled after a moment, she knew he had already forgiven her, but her apologising felt necessary.

"It was my fault" Elias told her guilty, "even if I didn't like what you wanted to do I shouldn't have said what I said. And I shouldn't have tried to stop you." His voice sincere, and Aloura almost found herself crying at the gentleness of his words.

"It's okay" Aloura smiled, "let's not talk about it."

Elias smiled at her with sad eyes, before lowering his lips to hers, offering her a quick peck before ushering her to a table in need of service.

♡ ♡ ♡

Aloura sat in the back booth waiting for Annie to be done with her shift, the papers of notes she'd made in front of her. Aloura didn't mind waiting, in fact, she found herself thankful for the extra moments she had to gather her thoughts. She had no idea what she wanted to ask, or if Annie would be any help. But for Elias, and justice for her mother, she was willing to try.

"Sorry I kept you waiting Bella" Annie sighed, as she slid into the booth. She placed her coat on the table, and her bag in her lap before looking up to Aloura's gentle smile. "You said you have some questions?"

Aloura thought for a moment before nodding, "it's about uh" Aloura used the pen to scratch her forehead, "my mother's death." Annie froze; Aloura had never wanted to talk about the accident before. At the start, she had even refused to believe she was dead. Talking about seeing her sitting in the stars or what not- Annie was shocked her father didn't send her to therapy.

Annie swallowed and nodded her head, "yes dear" she smiled, although Aloura could tell it was forced, "what about it."

Aloura turned the article page she had written out to face Annie, "I read that it says it wasn't an accident." Annie doesn't look down to the paper at first, probably because she knew this all along. "It also says here" Aloura pointed to the sheet of paper, "that it was related to a specific organisation. But you knew this. Right?"

Annie sighed, "I did."

"How is my mother connected to these people Annie?" Aloura's voice was desperate, and Agnus remembered her mother taking this exact same route. It was the curiosity that killed her.

"I promised her I would never tell" Annie's eyebrows furrowed as she swallowed, "you should stop searching Aloura, your mum took this same route a few years ago. And look where it led her."

Aloura ignored her statement, "you promised you'd never tell what? What route? Please stop talking in codes. I just want to know what she was involved with."

"It was her secret to-"

"It killed her Agnus!" Aloura snapped, "this secret took my mum, and I have a right to know it." Annie flinched at the name; yet she still watched the angry girl with loving eyes. She knew the ending of this story, she had watched it unfold before, and she didn't like how it ended. She only prayed that Aloura, and whoever she was trying to save, had a better ending.

Annie swallowed and nodded. "Very well" she muttered, her eyes fell to the table in concentration. "Your father always had a gambling problem."

Aloura frowned, that was something she had never known about Michael, but something she didn't find shocking to learn. "Even when I used to look after you, your parents would constantly argue about it. Your mother drew the line when he touched your college fund"

Aloura frowned, "he spent the rest of it after she died."

Agnus nodded meekly, "he had gambled all his money, and he turned to taking loans to save his marriage." Aloura swallowed, the story suddenly sounded familiar to one she'd heard a few nights ago. "They were sketchy people. Dute I think. They made them do all sorts to pay back their debt."

"Like what?"

"Your mother never said what they made him do" Agnus sighed, her fingers playing with the corner of the paper on the table. "But she found something" she couldn't believe she was telling the young girl all this; she was practically leading her to her death. "I'm not sure what, but she had begged me to watch out for you, telling me they were coming." Aloura didn't reply, her throat felt constricted. "I think she knew it was her end."

Aloura stared off behind Agnus' head, her mind racing to think of any unusual events during her childhood, but she came up empty handed. Aloura turned the sheet, so it faced her, "did she ever say anything about an offering?"

"An offering?" Agnus' eyebrows furrowed, deep in thought, before shaking her head, "not that I can remember." Aloura frowned before Annie spoke up again,

"She did once mention some type of eccentric payment"

Chapter Twenty Nine

Aloura pushed open the apartment door, a dwalm feeling permeated her body. She felt confused, lost even. It seemed like every time she uncovered something new, it only complicated matters more. Aloura shut the door behind her, before leaning against it, her eyes tightly shut. Something she wished she could do to the world around her.

Elias turned into the corridor after hearing the door open and no one walking in, he frowned at the sight of the stressed girl; his heart breaking into a million pieces. "Aloura?" he called out as he took steady steps towards her. His eyebrows knitted together when she made no efforts of concealing her dejection. She was fine at work, what could have flipped her mood so suddenly? "What wrong?" he asked, placing two hands on her deflated shoulders and looking down at her in worry.

Aloura exhaled and looked up at Elias, who could have sworn he could almost hear her brain spinning with thoughts. Aloura swallowed, "I spoke to Annie about my parents." She started, and Elias suddenly made sense of her behaviour, his heart going out to her. Sure, he had lost both his parents too, but he knew they were never coming back. Losing a parent to something other than death leaves room for yearn and hope, entrapping one into a cycle of disappointment. "She uh told me some stuff."

Elias nodded again with soft eyes, and Aloura placed her hand on her head, she needed to sit down, and Elias could see that. "Do you want to sit and talk down?" he offered and Aloura nodded, so Elias guided them to the couch, before taking a seat. "You told me about a Dr Lee on the rooftop that night." Aloura told him, Elias nodded, although it wasn't a question. "Dr Lee is my dad."

Elias' world stopped spinning and for a minute, and his eyebrows furrowed. He wanted to stand up, and swipe the table clean, ask Aloura how long she'd known this. But what difference would it have made. Would he have not taken her in because of her father's actions. Would his heart not miss a beat at the sound of her name had he knew. So instead, he closed his eyes and inhaled. Aloura reluctantly spoke again. "He used to gamble and took a loan from the Dute gang."

Elias' eyes flew open, and he sat up right. "How do you know about Dute?" his voice was low, but only because he was scared.

For himself, for Aloura and for whatever future they had, whether it be separate or apart.

Aloura sniffled, "they killed my mum." Elias had always known they were a brutal gang, after all they had threatened Kalian and Aloura life before, but he hadn't ever heard of a story where they followed their threats. Probably because they didn't live to tell the story.

That's how boss knew Aloura Elias thought. He turned his attention to Aloura, as if asking her why. Aloura shrugged at his silent question. "That's what I want to talk to my dad about."

Elias reluctantly nodded, not wanting a replay of last night events. "We have to stop them Elias." Aloura said after a moment, Elias' head snapped to hers, he scanned her face for a moment, in search of any indication of her joking. But he found none. Was she going crazy?

"They're an entire organisation Aloura, we wouldn't even stand a chance." Aloura knew this, so his words did nothing to deter the girl, instead, she just shrugged.

"On the rooftop we said we'd go to college; you want Kalian here. Don't you? Anything is worth what we stand to gain. What do you have to lose? A life that's not even yours because of them?" Aloura told him, she now sat at the edge of her seat, her hands grasping his forearm.

Elias looked down at her hand, and back at her, "we could die Aloura."

"*Anything* is worth what we stand to gain."

"Do you have a plan?" He asked after a moment of silence. He trusted Aloura, what she was saying was right. If they don't do anything now, Kalian will never come home, and Elias and Aloura would never go to college.

Aloura nodded, "I have some ideas." She grabbed her notes, and her mother's papers from her bag and turned them to him. Elias grabbed the papers and looked down at them.

"But I need to talk to my dad first. And I need your gun."

♡ ♡ ♡

Aloura flinched at the coldness of the doorknob as it shot through her arm, it felt numbing, and even after she had retracted her hand from it, its presence lingered. She pressed her hand onto her jeans, an unavailing attempt to heat it up.

The house was empty when she entered, and messier than it had ever been. But Aloura expected this, after all she was the only one who cared for the house, and with her absence, it was only a matter of time before it was damaged by her father. Another creation of her mother's destroyed at the hands of him. Aloura, being the first, of course.

Aloura walked through her old home like a stranger visiting for the first time, her eyes scanning every smashed photo on the floor, every discarded beer bottle and every hole in the wall. *I guess he needed something to get his anger out,* Aloura thought, suddenly regretting her decision of coming. *Elias was right, he's going to kill me.* Aloura turned to stare at the door, suddenly unsure if this was the right way about this. She stopped and thought for a moment before furrowing her eyebrows, *Elias and mother are worth losing my life for anyway.*

She nodded to herself, agreeing with her words silently, before turning away from the door. Instead, walking towards the staircase that led to her bedroom, shivering at her last memory in the house.

Her room was surprisingly untouched, everything was exactly where she'd left, including the pool of her own blood and the handprints where she'd begged to be let out. Aloura cringed at the sight, before stepping over the mess. She turned to her wardrobe and pulled out the remainder of her clothes, stuffing them into a backpack before zipping it up.

She placed the backpack on her shoulder and left the room, halting as she heard movement downstairs. She stood for a moment, listening in, before she began to walk towards the sound, she could practically feel her bones quaking against one another as she walked. The lump in her throat was growing by the second, and she found herself no longer feeling so brave.

Aloura hadn't reached the middle of the staircase when Michael spotted her, Aloura cursed her rattling bones that had given her away. He wasn't drunk, that was a first, Aloura thought as he took his steady steps towards her. "Aloura?" he called out to her, as if making sure she really was stood in front of him.

If Aloura was scared, she didn't let it show. Her face remained stoic as she lifted the hem of her shirt up, revealing the gun tucked in her waistband. Michaels' eyes widened, before taking a step back. "Me and you are going to have a *nice* chat" she sarcastically grinned at him. He stared at her but nodded leading the way to the living room.

Aloura remained standing at the doorway until her father sat down, and when he did she lifted her shirt slightly and retracted the gun. Elias had warned her how uncomfortable it was to sit with, and she wasn't all that keen to find out herself. at the sight of the gun, Michael raised his hands, mumbling a 'woah woah.'

Aloura ignored him, she placed the gun under her thigh and grabbed her papers. "There's two ways this can go." She told him, finally looking up to meet his alarmed gaze. "One: you give all the answers I need, and you walk out scot free. Or Two: Katherine Kader's son can come here and get the answers from you that way." Michael's eyes widened at the name of his victim, and at the fact his daughter knew he had any victims.

Aloura shifted uncomfortably in her seat, her tough demeaner was hard to keep when all she wanted to do was cry and ask him why he ever hurt her. She had no intention of hurting him, or allowing Elias to hurt him, but he didn't need to know that. When Michael didn't reply, Aloura carried on. "What did you have to do with Dute?"

Michael swallowed and looked around the apartment with wide eyes, Aloura was going to get them all killed; Dute had ears everywhere. "I took a loan from them." he told her after a moment of uncomfortable silence, "the agreement was I take the money, pay the mortgage and the bills, and I'd pay them back when I had the money." Aloura didn't reply to him, part of her was shocked he'd answered.

When Aloura didn't reply, he continued. "Fuckers showed up one night, asking for every penny I'd took and the interest. And I didn't have it to give." He winced at the memory of his wife and him being held at gun point. "They said they could shoot everyone in the house as payment, or I'd work for them." He ran a hand over his almost bald head. "Naturally, I agreed."

Aloura scoffed, although she would have done the same. "They cancelled your debt because you worked for them?"

Michael inhaled, his head now hanging low, almost like he was embarrassed or regretful of his actions. "It wasn't any type of work Aloura" he cautioned, "it was their dirty work."

Aloura had figured that much, after all it was an entire gang. "What did they make you do?

"All sorts" his voice trembled. "The main thing they'd ask for was customers."

"Customers?"

He nodded meekly, "Those with no insurance. Or who's insurance wouldn't cover their treatment." His eyes seemed distant, "they'd tell me who, and what to say. I just had to be the doctor that approached them and lead them to Dute."

It had all fallen to place for Aloura now. Her father was forced to make up fake treatments and offer them to vulnerable people and families. And when the family would mention how they were unable to afford the treatment, her father would introduce them to Dute. Thus, entrapping more people, like Elias and his family in their sick scheme.

"You've ruined so many people's lives." Aloura told him, but he knew that. Memories of what he'd done kept him up at night, even drinking couldn't seem to help him escape from them demons. Michael didn't reply, only hanging his head lower in shame. "Did mum know?"

Michael shook his head, his body tense "she knew I took a loan from sketchy people after they'd barged into the house." Aloura listened intently, "but I'd never told her how I had to pay them back."

"Did she ever find out?" he nodded at this, and Aloura sighed, shifting in her seat.

"She demanded I'd find a way to stop, or she was going to take the whole organisation down." He laughed at this, like something was funny. "She was a single person" he shook his head, but Aloura could see the tears that threatened to spill from his eyes. "She stood no chance."

"She was brave." Aloura seethed, and Michael laughed again.

"What good is bravery if it kills you?" Aloura paused, his words sinking deep in her and striking a chord.

"Do you call this living?" Aloura sneered gesturing to the run down home. "Is this how good your cowardice is?"

Michael didn't reply, but maybe because Aloura left no room for a discussion. "You said she wanted you to find a way out." Michael nodded again, "did you?" Aloura watched as his head bobbed again. "Does it have anything to do with an eccentric payment?"

His eyes peeled in shock, "how do you" he stammered, before swallowing, "how do you know about that?"

"Answer the question Michael, I don't have time." She snapped, her hand moving under her thigh, a silent reminder that she still had a gun.

"Aloura. You remind me of your mother in many ways." Aloura's mouth felt dry, "but this is what killed her. Why do you want to take the same route she did?"

Aloura dismissed his words, she wished she was half the woman her mother was, "you said something about an offering and it being my fault. What did you mean?'

Michael sighed, running a hand down his face, "Aloura, please drop this."

"You have five fucking seconds to start talking before I either shoot your brains out, or Katherine Kader's son does."

Michael gulped, he had no interest in meeting an angry victim of his, but he had no interest in dying by the hands of Dute boss' either. When he didn't start speaking, Aloura lifted the gun, using the thumb lever to eject the magazine. She showed him the loaded magazine, a daring look in her eyes. She fed the magazine back into the gun, and Michael flinched at the sound of a live round now in the chamber.

 "I thought the eccentric payment was the way out" his voice shook, and his eyes remained trained on the gun. Aloura was almost scared he'd notice how much it shook in her hand. "I just had to make it look like an accident and use your life insurance to pay off the debt."

"You were going to have me killed off?" Aloura laughed, despite finding nothing funny in the situation. Michael nodded again meekly; his shoulders slumped.

"They said they'd deal with everything, and I- we would be free." Aloura licked her bottom lip, suddenly angry her father had made a life without her in it. "But your mother found out."

"She offered herself instead of me?' Aloura whispered, her hands visibly trembling now.

"She changed the papers behind my back." Michael coughed into his locked fist. Aloura scanned his appearance quickly, he looked worse than the last time she saw him. She mentally scoffed, how did her beautiful mama end with a guy like this? "I never wanted this to happen-"

"Is my life insurance still active?" Aloura cut him off, her finger hovering over the trigger. She had long filled the vacant space he had left; she was no longer interested in mending whatever relationship they had. Aloura sighed in relief at her fathers timid 'yes'.

"Who did you contact to organise the eccentric payment?"

Chapter Thirty

Aloura slipped through the apartment door, discarding her bag and coat onto the hangers before walking deeper into the home. The smell of cooking had hit her as soon as she entered the door. She smiled; *I could get used to this.* "Aloura?" Elias called from the kitchen.

She pulled a fake face and skipped to where his voice sounded, her heart exploding at the sight of him cooking. Aloura laughed when he'd turned to face her, he had managed to somehow get more food onto his apron than on the dish. "Woah did you leave any to actually eat?" she joked, Elias laughed, throwing an apron in her face.

"I didn't tie mine, look" he grinned at her, turning around to show her in case she didn't believe him. "We gotta do each other's again."

Aloura's grin matched his as she slipped the apron hoop through her neck. She grabbed the strings attached on Elias' apron and paused for a moment, racking her brain for the steps she'd mastered this morning. She hooped the strings before knotting them together. She frowned a little at its abnormal look, but it was short lived as Elias cheered. "You actually remembered!" Elias encouraged, a proud smile tugging at his lips. The praise from Elias, although over something feeble, spilled into her body and made a home in her chest. She grinned up at him and turned around.

Elias held her strings and looped them, "How was the talk with your dad?" he asked the dreaded question. Aloura bit her lip, and her eyes found the floor. Elias knotted the loops and placed his hands on Aloura's hips, spinning her around. His hands remained on her hips, and he stared down at her with concerned eyes.

"I was right. He is the same Dr that got you in this mess" she told him; her heart heavy. "He took a loan and was forced to pay it back by preying on vulnerable people in the hospital." She watched as Elias' jaw clenched. "I'm sorry"

Elias shook his head and swallowed his tears, "it's not your fault" his voice strained but sincere. "Did he give you any information on how to get out this mess?" he handed Aloura the chopping board and freshly washed vegetables.

Aloura placed the pepper on the board, "no" the sound of the knife hitting the board echoed through the kitchen.

"No more secrets?" he whispered to her after a moment. Aloura stared up at him and smiled, her gaze fell to his hand as she pried it from his face. Elias frowned at her, "what're you doing?"

"it's a pinkie promise" Aloura laughed lightly.

I don't believe in promises. I don't believe in promises. Aloura lifted the knife and cut the pepper again, her mind lost in thought. I don't believe in promises. Cut. I don't believe in promises. *You shouldn't have lied. You agreed to no more secrets.* She thought to herself, she shook her head. *No. I'm only trying to help.*

"Aloura?" Elias pried the knife out her hands, his eyebrows knitted. "Are you okay?"

"Yeah, yeah sorry" Aloura muttered and wiped her hands down her apron, Elias watched her for a moment before nodding.

"Why don't you just sit and watch me cook tonight?"

♡ ♡ ♡

Elias placed a plate of lasagne in front of a grinning Aloura, before taking a seat across from her. He pulled his chair into the table and looked to meet Aloura's stare. "How is it?" he asks. Aloura places a forkful in her mouth, Elias watching her do so. She chewed slowly; her face neutral. "You're killing me" he laughed.

Aloura bit back her grin and pulled a funny face. "It's good" she wheezed out sarcasm dripping from her words and spilling on the table. Aloura almost felt bad when Elias pulled a heartbroken look, before looking down at his food. "Do you want me to make you something else?' he pulled his hair back, "there's not much left in the kitchen so it won't be much-"

Aloura cut him off by falling into a fit of giggles. "I was kidding" she laughed. He frowned at her, not believing her words. "I promise, look" she grabbed another forkful and placed it in her mouth. Elias scowled at her.

"You scared me" he told her, pushing his chair back into the wooden table.

Aloura scoffed, "not my fault you're not confident in your abilities." She forked another bite into her mouth and grinned at Elias.

Elias lifted his glass of water to his lips and watched Aloura. "Finish your food and I'll show you which abilities I'm confident in," he smirked.

Aloura's eyes widened, coughing hysterically at his sudden change of topic, her mind racing to the ways he made her feel last time. Elias held her stare as he pushed his glass of water to her gently, "save the chocking for later" he chuckled, before sitting back in his chair.

Aloura didn't reply, instead, she reached for the water and took large gulps, a feeble attempt to quench her thirst. But it wasn't water she needed. The pair ate in silence for the remainder of the night, stealing occasional glances at each other in anticipation of what would happen after.

Aloura's mind alternated to wanting to scarf down the food to speed the process or taking as long as humanely possible to prologue this night forever. Elias finished his dinner before

Aloura did. He stood silently and took his dishes to the sink, before turning the faucet on.

Aloura shoved the remainder of her food in her mouth, before collecting her own cutlery. She made her way to Elias, who turned and took the dirty dishes from her, "oh no, it's okay" Aloura smiled at him, "I can wash my plate."

Elias shook his head and took the plate before placing it in the sink, "why don't you just wait in the room?" he whispered, causing a shiver of excitement to run down Aloura's back. Aloura stared at him for a moment before giving him a silent nod; not moving out the kitchen until Elias had turned back around to wash their plates.

Aloura bit back a grin as she grabbed her backpack from the hanger in the hallway, slipping silently into the bathroom. She spilled her clothes onto the floor and stood above them. She furrowed her eyebrows at the lack of variety she had. She ran a hand through her locks before lowering herself onto the ground. She lifted a few pairs and threw them into the dismissal pile. She didn't have many options but had always attempted to spice her sex life with Kaden up. Key word being attempted. Aloura was pulled out her trance at the sound of Elias' knocks on the door. "You okay in there?" he called out.

Aloura nodded before realising he couldn't see her, "uh yeah I'll be there in a second." Elias gave her a small okay, before retreating into the bedroom. Aloura looked at the pile of clothes before spotting a pair. She grinned and grabbed the matching set before slipping it on. She lifted the rest of her clothes back into the backpack. With unsteady hands she unlocked the bathroom door before following Elias' footsteps into the room. Her hands tightened around the backpack handle as she stood in Elias' line of vision. Elias locked his phone and tore his eyes up to meet Aloura's figure, his breath hitching at the sight of her.

Elias used his hands to push his body onto the edge of the bed but remained seated. He threw his phone to the side, his eyes never leaving Aloura. He reached out to her, prying the backpack from her hands and discarding it before holding her hand gently and pulling her into him.

He held her at arm's length, his eyes scanning every part of her. Aloura bit her lip anxiously, both regretful for trying so hard and excited. Elias swallowed and he placed his hands on Aloura's hips. The exposed skin where he touched burned in desperation, and Aloura fought the urge of grabbing his hands and making him touch her everywhere.

Elias gripped her hip, using it to guide Aloura around, spinning her slowly. Aloura didn't resist his wordless commands, she turned for him, and Elias admired her silently. He sucked in a lungful of air as she turned back around to face him, "and just when I thought you couldn't get any more beautiful."

Aloura blushed at his words, but offered him no reply, instead, she leaned down into him and pressed her lips onto his. Elias wasn't complaining, he'd missed the feeling of her mouth on his. He pressed his hand flat on her cheek, and she placed her hands on his chest to steady herself, her knees suddenly weak from the touch of him.

Elias' lips moved against Aloura's, this time less gentle, but still loving. the sensation of his lips sent jitters into her stomach. His togue brushed her bottom lip, pressing it into her mouth, their lips now moving in unison. Aloura pulled away gently, yearning for air. Elias panted, and reached for Aloura's body, drawing her into his arms and onto his lap. The legs of Aloura now draped on either side of his body, their lips interlocked once again.

Elias had rested his hands on Aloura's hips, firmly holding her in his lap, before lowering them to reach for her arse. Aloura lets out a moan as his hands gripped her and squeezed her tightly. She lifts her arms to the length of Elias' shirt, and he instantaneously pulls away to allow her to remove it.

She drops his shirt onto the floor carelessly before gently sucking on his collar bone with her lips. The love bites from before were faint, yet still noticeable. Aloura pulled her lips away from Elias' body and buried them on his. His hands reached for Aloura's breasts, slipping them under her bra and tightly grasping them. He groaned at the annoying fabric restricting his movement, so he unclasped her and slid it off her body in one swift sweep. Discarding on the floor, next to his shirt.

Elias moves down to her now- exposed chest and catches an erect nipple in between his lips, teasing it with his tongue. Aloura whimpered in response and pushed her hips against Elias' crotch, eagerly grinding against him in search of any kind of release. Elias' hands halted her lips firmly, he dropped her rosy tips from his mouth and lifted Aloura gently. Aloura followed his actions, her body now hovering over his as he pulled down his sweatpants. He kicked them off his ankles and pressed Aloura back down onto him. Aloura placed her hands flat onto his chest, gently pushing him back onto the bed. He held her hips and pulled them further up the bed, his body now propped slightly up by the pillows.

Elias let Aloura take control, he loved the view of her over him anyway.

Chapter Thirty One

Aloura leaned in close to Elias' chest, leaving a trail of hickies on his golden skin. Elias swallowed and stared at the scene in front of him with hungry eyes; Aloura was beautiful clothed, he had thought that from the moment he saw her. But she looked like a goddess nude.

Aloura pulled at Elias' boxers as he reached to the bed side table for a condom. He sat back in his place and faced Aloura- holding out the packaging in his hand. Aloura didn't take it from his hands, instead, she leaned over, and with her eyes locked onto his, she placed the corner of the package in her mouth. She placed her hand on his pelvis to steady herself as she ripped the package open with her teeth. Elias licked his bottom lip but said nothing. Too fearful his dry mouth would betray him.

Aloura grabbed the condom from him, before scooting back down to her previous position, and Elias watched her breasts bounce at her movement, shifting in his place. Aloura grabbed his girth and placed a few strokes on his dick before situating the condom at his tip, evoking a string of moans.

After securing it on, Aloura lifted her hand to her mouth and spat twice, before lowering her hand onto Elias' dick, lathering her spit around. Elias once again shifted in his place, grunting in pleasure. Aloura abandoned his crotch and scooted up, pressing her lips on him gently. Elias used one hand to grab her throat, squeezing it lightly as their lips connected. A few seconds later, and Aloura broke the kiss, moving back down Elias' body.

Elias held Aloura's waist and held her up as she grabbed the hem of her underwear and slipped them off. They were pretty, but an unnecessary hinderance between them. Aloura discarded them next to their other clothes, before turning to Elias. His hand moved slowly to the slit of her jewel, inserting his fingers gently. Aloura tensed but gave him way. He curled his finger inside her, inserting and retracting them for a few times before pulling away. He placed his fingers at the bundle of nerves between her legs, her wetness on his fingers as lubrication.

Aloura swallowed and held his shaft and positioned herself above it before lowering herself down slowly. If Elias was sexually frustrated by her slow pace, he didn't show it. Instead, he helped hold her up with one hand, and the other massaging her bud of nerves.

Aloura rocked and swayed back and forth on Elias' shaft, prompting him to utter a torrent of curse words. Her stomach churned with the sensation of being full. Seemingly growing dissatisfied with her hesitation, and slow pace, Elias placed both hands on her hips, forcing her down as he thrust up, sending Aloura into a fit of whimpers.

"Fuck" he moaned into her ear, *"you feel so good, Aloura."*

♡ ♡ ♡

The space beside Elias had long grown cold when he'd rolled into it in the morning. He groaned and stretched, before he grabbed the pillow underneath his head and wrapped it around his face, annoyed at the light that infiltrated the room.

He blinked a couple of times before he dropped the pillow and lifted his head, his eyes scanned the room for a certain green eyed brunette. His stomach clenched when he found no sight of her. He threw the covers off his body in a haste, before grabbing his discarded boxers and sweats and pulling them on.

He briskly opened his bedroom door and stepped into the hallway; his lips suddenly dry at the thought of Aloura disappearing. His erratic heart only calmed after he walked into the kitchen, spotting a silent Aloura sat on the kitchen table, one of her legs propped up, and her arm wrapped around it securely. She had rested her head on her knee, deep in thought as she spilled her thoughts into the paper.

She wore Elias' shirt from last night, it had ridden up slightly, showcasing her underwear band. He sighed in relief and approached her cautiously. He gently placed his hand onto her back, rubbing it gently. Only then did Aloura notice his presence. She flinched and squealed slightly, before looking up at Elias, "you scared me" she laughed, although he could tell by her reaction.

Elias smiled at her, before pecking her grin softly, "sorry baby." He pulled the seat beside her and motioned to the sheet of paper, "what you writing?"

Aloura's eyes looked around for an excuse, she shrugged and turned the sheet around. "Issa' secret."

Elias frowned at her; he didn't like the sound of that. "You can't keep secrets from me, we made a *pinkie* promise" he told her, placing extra enunciation on the pinkie, in case she forgot she stood at a chance of losing her pinkie.

Aloura laughed at this, "I'll tell you soon I promise." He frowned but dropped it, he trusted her.

Elias stood from the table and walked around the kitchen island and to the kettle. He flicked it on and opened the cupboard, grabbing two mugs if coffee. "Do you have plans today?" he turned to Aloura, who had placed her head back on her knees, admiring the shirtless tan brunette as he worked.

Aloura shook her head as she watched Elias scoop the coffee and into the mugs, "we've not been to the roof top in a while" she told him.

Elias grabbed the kettle and poured the hot water into the cups, "do you want to go today?" he grabbed the milk and poured it in their cups.

"Can we?"

"We can do anything you like" he told her, handing her a mug. She grinned at him and muttered a 'thanks.' He kissed her forehead and took the place beside her.

"We can finish the book today!" Aloura cheered, her eyes lighting up at the thought of finally reaching the end. They had religiously read together each night, a perfect and cheap substitute to watching rentals. Something they both refused to waste money on. Plus, Elias didn't have a tv.

Elias grinned, "yeah but I'm not starting because I read more last time."

Aloura frowned and pouted, she did not like the sound of that, "but I like listening to you read." Elias closed his eyes. He didn't want to see the innocent look she would shoot at him; he knew he'd give into her. "Please, please, please" she begged, shaking his arm.

He peeled an eye open and sighed, "you're lucky you're cute." He told her, she lifted the mug to her lips, a forlorn attempt to hide the smug grin inscribed on her face. "Before we go, can we talk more about whatever your plan is?" Elias placed his arms on the table.

Aloura swallowed but nodded, "sure, what's up?"

"Talk me through everything. Please."

Aloura watched him for a moment but nodded, she thanked the skies that she had prepared for his questions. She stood from the table and walked to her bag, before spilling the pages on the table. "When's your next fight?" she asked, Elias frowned before answering.

"Tomorrow."

Aloura's breath hitched in her mouth, and the lump in her throat tightened. Aloura pushed through it and blinked rapidly. "And the boss will be there?" Elias nodded again, Aloura looked at him for a moment. "We need to get him in a room." Elias' eyebrows knitted together, and he parted his lips to object, but Aloura was quick to shush him, "You'll be there I promise." When her words did nothing to reassure him, she placed her hand gently on his. "Don't worry Eli. Think about calling Kalian after and telling him the good news."

Elias nodded reluctantly, he trusted her. Aloura carried on, "when we have him in a room, we have to keep him there. Until the authorities come"

"I have the evidence of all the patient confidentiality violations and the fraud." Aloura handed him the sheets, he flicked through them, his heart sinking at his own mother's documents in the pile. "And then" Aloura paused looking around the table for a specific piece of paper. She shuffled the sheets around and picked up the small note with a list of names her mother had written. She handed it to Elias, "we call up and report to both the list."

"Why?"

"My mother said one of them is corrupt and part of the organisation but didn't specify which. By calling both, the odds are in our favour." Elias listened intently, he didn't like the sound of gambling with their life, but this was barely living.

"And then we're free?" Elias' voice mumbled; vulnerability evident in his voice.

"And then we're free." She told him, *"I pinkie promise Eli."*

Chapter Thirty Two

Elias placed the small picnic blanket in their designated corner as Aloura unpacked their dinner. They had, after Aloura's constant nagging, agreed to spend the majority of the night, and have dinner on the rooftop. Like the older days, as Aloura had described it. Although it wasn't that long ago.

Elias would never admit it, but he too liked the sound of spending the day at the rooftop. It was, when with Aloura, a safe space. Although he knew that really meant Aloura was his safe space.

Aloura reached for their book from the bottom of her bag and held it excitedly, waiting for Elias to sit down so she could take her place between his legs. Elias laughed at the impatient look she shot him but said nothing as he took a seat. Aloura didn't give him time to position himself comfortably, before she practically threw herself onto him. Elias grunted at the impact but steadied her, "easy there tiger."

Aloura shot him an apologetic grin before turning and pressing her back into his stomach. Elias pressed his lips against her hair and smiled, before placing a small kiss. Aloura pried open the book and found where they'd left off, before handing it to him. "We gotta finish it tonight" she told him, he frowned down at her even though she couldn't see him.

"And why's that?" Aloura shrugged, although she knew why. Elias laughed against her hair, "whatever you want princess."

Elias held open the book and read aloud as the smaller girl rested her head against his shoulder. A small smile grazing her lips. She felt peaceful, she felt at home. "Eli" she called for him, he paused his reading and hummed in response. "You said you wanted to make a home with me one day." Aloura felt him nod his head softly, "you made a home in my heart. And nothing that could happens tomorrow will ever change that."

Elias smiled and kissed her hair, "you have a home in my heart too baby."

Aloura's lip quivered, and tears filled her eyes, her eyes flew to the lone star that blinked the brightest in the sky, "my mum would have loved you." Elias swallowed the growing lump in his throat, her words meant the world to him.

"My parents would have loved you too" he told her sincerely, tears now filled his own eyes at the memory of his parents. "Especially my mum."

"Really?" Aloura sniffles, he nods. "Can I meet them?"

Elias frowned for a moment, thinking her words were some sort of sick joke, before realising. his eyes rise to the two stars sat together, glistening back at the rooftop. He clears his throat. "Mum, dad this is Aloura." He tells them, feeling a little stupid. He paused for a moment, realising his words had somehow closed a gaping hole in his chest. "Aloura, those are my parents. Katherine and Marcus Kader."

Aloura smiled at the skies, muttering a small hello, "My mum's called Dara West" she told the stars, "You guys should find her and get to know each other until we come."

Elias laughs at this but nods his head softly in agreement as a tear rolled his cheek. They watch the stars in silence for a moment, as if waiting for a reply.

"I feel guilty that I don't go to my mother's grave." Aloura confessed after a moment, "I feel like I owe it to her to at least make it pretty."

"Why don't you go?" he mumbles back.

"it's too painful" she confesses, "sitting amongst the sea of graves reminds me how truly irrelevant her death was to everyone else. I like the rooftop because I can pretend for a moment, she's alive even if she's not with me- she's out there. But her grave reminds me she's dead."

Elias nods, "I understand." He reassures her, "and so does she."

Aloura's eyes fly to the star at the mention of her. "Do you visit your parents' graves?' she asks. Elias nods again.

"I used to go almost every day." He forces out, "I found it therapeutic to rant to them."

"What were they like?" Aloura asks, turning her head to side to look at him. Elias forces out a sad chuckle.

"My mum was an angel with no wings." He smiled at the memory, "I used to be convinced that God sent her without them as a disguise. I still am, except she has wings now" Aloura laughed sadly at this. "She used to be so patient." He thinks for a moment before forcing out another laugh, "So patient." He repeats sadly, his voice now much quieter.

Aloura runs her hand comfortingly on his thigh, he looks down at it. "There's no nice way to say this but my dad was one son of a bitch. But I loved him." Elias wiped the tear that fell from his eye. "When he died, I used to sit at his grave and talk to him to spite him."

Aloura frowned at this, "what do you mean?"

"He was one stubborn mother fucker" Elias laughed, "his word always had to be the last. I was angry that he had left me and Kalian." He picked a bit of fluff from the blanket beneath him, "mainly Kalian." Aloura nodded, and rubbed his thigh again, this time bringing her hand to his knee and drawing small circles with her index finger. He tore his eyes from Aloura's hand on his knee and looked at the stars.

"Talking to his gravestone was the only time I ever got a word in with him."

♡ ♡ ♡

Elias lifted his fork into Aloura's mouth, she bit on it. Elias grinned and shook it as her teeth were still clamped around it- only to be annoying of course. Aloura glared at him and chewed her food, she grabbed a forkful of her own lasagne that they had reheated from last night and placed it at Elias' mouth.

Elias looked at her suspiciously. He had just messed with her, and Aloura took getting even extremely seriously. Aloura held her free hand up in surrender. "I'm not gonna do anything I swear."

He eyed her for a moment before going to bite down on the fork, but Aloura was quick to move it away. She fell into a fit of giggles as Elias threw her an unamused look "hey!" he cried. "You promised you wasn't gonna do anything." He told her.

"Nu uh" Aloura frowned, "I *swore*. There's a difference."

Elias scoffed, "No there isn't, you're just a cheater."

Aloura laughed and placed the fork back at the entrance of his mouth. "I'm serious this time. I won't do anything."

Elias frowned at her before grabbing her wrist and holding it in place, and only after securing it, he took the food. Grinning with pride, Aloura laughed at him, but said nothing. Silence settled over the pair as they ate their food under the moons light. Aloura swallowed her bite and looked at Elias, "Are we friends?" she asked him randomly.

He frowned at her words- did she let friends fuck her like he did? "I think we're a little more than friends." He told her gently, swallowing the jealousy that bubbled inside of him at the thought of another touching her.

Aloura nodded and smiled, "I want to be a lot more than friends" she confessed, her face beetroot red.

Elias grinned at her adorable nature, 'Then we're a lot more than friends." Aloura's grinned matched his. "After tomorrow is over, I'll take you on a date" he promised her. Aloura's smile faltered slightly, but he missed it.

"I can't wait" she told him.

Elias smiled at the girl who sat Criss-crossed a few inches away from him, "Me too baby."

He placed the lid on his now empty container and fished for his phone in his pocket. He frowned at the time, before looking up to Aloura, "We should head back and sleep sweetheart, its elven and we have a big day tomorrow."

"But we didn't finish the book yet" she pouted at him, he laughed and kissed her pout.

"I'll read it to you tomorrow baby, I promise."

Aloura looked behind her at the star, then back at Elias and nodded, a small smile tugging at her lips. "Okay."

Chapter Thirty Three

Aloura's leg bounced frantically as she awaited Elias. The coffee in her hands had long gone cold, and she could have sworn the butter on her toast had become rancid too. Yet, her mind was preoccupied with thoughts of what was to come, and the food in front of her was the least of her qualms.

It was only noon, but what was to come at midnight was sending the girls mind into a frenzy of anxiety. Not that she had regretted her decision of course, but she still couldn't shake the feelings of unease that filled the pits of her stomach. Aloura placed the cold cup of coffee on the kitchen table, fearful her shaking hands no longer had the strength to keep it steady. She walked towards her backpack and retreated a small note she had spent her time perfecting,. She looked down at it and pushed the choking feeling that had risen her throat.

Elias' approaching footsteps had broken her from her trance. She turned to face him, smiling lightly. Elias grinned back and took steady steps towards her, pressing his lips softly against his forehead as he fumbled with his shirt buttons. Aloura laughed at his struggles and dropped the note on the couch before turning to him. Her hands gently did up his buttons as he watched down at her lovingly. "Are you scared?" he asked, his voice gentle. Aloura shook her head, and he swallowed. "I am" he confessed.

"I know you're going to be okay, so I'm not scared." She told him as she finished doing up his buttons.

Elias smiled at her gently, "After this, we'll go to college together" Aloura laughed, "and then we'll ask each other, like we planned all along. Right?"

Aloura smiled gently and nodded, "I'll finally get to save people."

"You've already saved me"

Aloura stands on her tip toes and kisses his lips, *I hope so.* "Oh yeah" she grins before turning around and grabbing the note, she looks at them one last time before handing them to him.

"what's this?"

"Open it when we're finally out of there." She tells him, he grins and runs his finger across his name engraved in small handwriting. Suddenly feeling bad that he didn't get her anything, but vows in his head that as soon as this is over, he would buy her the earth and all its stars. "Come on baby, Blayde's waiting." She slips her hand into his and intertwines their fingers.

Elias tucks the note into his coat pocket and smiles at Aloura. They walk towards the door, and Elias raises their hands and places a small kiss on the back of Aloura's. She looks up at him and blushes.

I can't wait to love you.

♡ ♡ ♡

"You gotta stay hid in here until the fight is over, okay?" Elias asks as he lifts his water bottle to his mouth. Aloura nods, "I'm serious Aloura, Blayde will get the boss into the spare room, and I'll come get you and we go together." Aloura nods.

"I know Elias, I pinkie promise." She smiles and holds out her pinkie. He exhales and watches her finger warily before wrapping his own around it. He smiles gently, the pinkie promise seemingly reassuring him.

"Just a few more hours and we're free" he grins at her, although technically Aloura was already free- it was only his mess. Aloura laughs at this.

"I can't wait for Kalian to find out he's coming back." She grins, and Elias kisses her smile.

"He's going to be so excited."

Aloura smiles at him, "It'll all be worth it in the end." She grabs his hand wrap from the bench and unrolls it. "You gotta win your last fight or I'll pretend I don't know you."

Elias laughs, his eyes trained on her hands as they delicately wrapped his wrists. "Don't worry, you're my lucky charm remember." Aloura laughs and wraps his knuckles before moving it to the anchor of his thumb. "Blayde's going to keep an eye on the boss all night." He tells her, "To make sure he stays until the end."

Aloura nods and they settle into the silence as she finishes wrapping his hands up. He kisses her lips as a thank you. Blayde walks into the locker room and grins at the pair, "if it isn't my favourite single lady" Elias shoots him a disapproved look and Aloura laughs.

Elias slips his boxing gloves on as Blayde keeps talking, "This fucker really is taking his time huh?" he nodded his head to Aloura as they watched him. Although Aloura didn't know If he meant Elias was taking his time to get ready or making it official with her.

Elias shook his legs as he walked to them, he lifted his arm and punched Blayde lightly in the chest. Well, only Elias thought of it as light. "Step away from my girl Steel"

Aloura laughed and turned to Blayde, "Your second name is Steel?"

Blayde glared at Elias who laughed, "yeah I think my parents hate me" Aloura laughs again.

"It's okay, my second name is a cardinal direction."

They share a laugh again before Blayde taps Elias' shoulder, "Give this fine *single* lady your goodbyes and let's go. You're on in five minutes."

Elias punches Blayde's retreating figure again, who scowls and rubs his shoulder as he walks off. Elias turns to Aloura as the sound of the door closing echoes through the locker room. He smiles gently, "I'll come get you, okay?" he reminds her, she nods again. "Next time I see you, we'll be out this mess." He grins and Aloura matches it.

Elias' eyes flicker between Aloura's, he presses his lips onto hers gently, before pressing them against her forehead, "stay safe" he tells her, resisting the urge to say I love you.

Aloura nods, and blinks the tears away, "you too."

Elias takes in her look one last time before turning to the door, he stops and stands there for a moment, before jogging back turning back to Aloura. She offers him a perplexed look, but he kisses it away.

"I just wanted one more kiss" she laughs but gives him another. He grins and walks to the door, this time disappearing out of it.

Aloura instantaneously takes a seat and exhales, before placing a hand on her erratic heart. She pulls out her phone and the sheet of paper with names on them, she flips it and looks at the two numbers. She dials the first one.

"My mother left me a note with your name and number" she tells the person on the other end as soon as they answered. "It's about taking down Dute."

They ask for more information, and she gives them the address and asks them to hurry before hanging up. She closes her eyes and leans against the wall for a moment before dialling the other number and asking of them the same thing.

They hang up, and Aloura lifts her feet onto the bench before tucking her face into her knees. She lays her head to the side and lifts her phone, but she was only meant to call two numbers.

Aloura's fingers hover over the last number, she presses her eyes tightly shut and dials the number her father had given her. It rings twice, before picking up. But the person on the other end doesn't speak up. Aloura swallows.

"My name is Aloura West, and I want to set up an eccentric payment to write off Elias Kader."

Chapter Thirty Four

Blayde had two jobs. One, watch Elias's fight. Two, watch the boss. He had almost successfully done both when he watched the boss get a call. He frowned, praying on every star that he wasn't needed elsewhere. He had to stay in the building until the FBI and the two groups of enforcement officers made it here.

He looked to Elias who had thrown a punch at his opponent, making him lose his balance. His eyes find the timer behind him, they were on their third and last round, with less than a minute to go.

Blayde cursed as he watched the boss stand, his two men following suit. He jumped off his podium and walked to the boss' figure, pushing people hastily out the way. They called out to him with every curse word under the sun, but he paid no mind to them.

Elias threw another punch knocking the skinnier guy out, and the bell rang out before cheers filled the room. Elias grinned, Aloura really was his lucky charm. He turned with a large smile to where

Blayde had been standing but frowned when he saw he was no longer there.

The referee helped the other guy up and guided them to the middle of the ring. Elias' eyes scanned the room, he didn't care that he had just won, he needed to find his friend, or the entire plan would fall through. The crowd cheered, but Elias' had missed it due to his ringing ears. He almost didn't feel the referee lifting his hand up either, indicating he had won.

Elias looked at his raised hand, and then into the crowd, sighting in relief as he saw Blayde's figure following the boss that had just left the room.

Elias' heart skipped a beat as he noticed where he was leading too.

"Aloura" he muttered, almost like he had to say it aloud for his ears to believe she was in danger. He swore and pried his grip from the referee before walking to the edge of the ring.

He spotted Blayde's figure pushing back one of the boss' men in the doorway. He swallowed and jogged towards them. "You can't come through" he heard the suited man say. Elias scoffed and pushed passed Blayde. He grabbed the man's collared shirt and stepped into his face.

"Step the fuck out our way." He ordered; the men shook their heads.

"We can't" he told them, "Boss' orders." Elias scoffed again, before going to punch him. He halted at the door that burst open, and the police that filled the room.

♡ ♡ ♡

Aloura's curled body shot up from the bench as a masked man, and four suited men entered the door. "So, this is the brave Aloura West?" he laughed through his mask. Aloura swallowed.

"Who are you?" she asked. But she knew who out of the three phone calls would arrive first.

The man grinned, but it wasn't a sweet grin like Elias'. This one made her stomach nauseous. "Since you won't be alive for much longer, I'll introduce myself" he taunted her. She didn't reply, she didn't want to know his name.

"I'm Dene Mullin. You know it almost feels like I've had this conversation with your mother" he laughed. "Or is she alive?"

Aloura didn't reply, maybe because she knew that he knew her mother was dead, or because her mind was now focussed on the commotion outside. Her eyes snapped to the door at the sound of Elias' angry voice.

No Aloura cried in her head, *he can't see this.*

"Do you have the papers?" he walked towards her, and Aloura watched the door for a moment before nodding and walking to the bench. She lifted them and turned to him.

"Stay the fuck away from her" Elias' figure called from the door; his gloves were missing but his hand wraps remained on. His eyes widening at the sight of Aloura approaching their boss. "Aloura what're you doing."

Blayde now also came to view, and Aloura swallowed the lump in her throat, accidentally pushing her words down instead. Dene laughed and looked at his men who stood with stoic expressions. He nodded to the door and turned to Aloura.

Aloura watched with wide eyes as two men each grabbed Elias and Blayde. They struggled in the men's' holds. Aloura turned to Dene. "Please, let them go. You can't hurt them."

Dene laughed, "Sure I can. You're not dead yet so he" he turned and nodded to a frantic Elias, "still belongs to me."

Elias froze at the words, and his eyes met Aloura's "what?" his voice was above a whisper, and Aloura's eyes filled with tears. His eyes held hurt, and she was sure if Dene didn't kill her fast, Elias' heartbroken look would.

Aloura was the first to break the stare, she turned to dene. "So, kill me" her voice didn't shake, but her heart did.

"Fuck. No. Aloura." Elias cried as the men tightened their hold on him. "The police are here. They'll take them all down baby. Don't do this." But Aloura shook her head at him, the police were corrupt. Why couldn't he understand?

Aloura's lips quivered as she looked at Elias, "You have to get Kalian" she told him, "And go to college. Okay?"

"We'll get Kalian together baby and go to college together. Like we said we would. Don't do this. The police will be here any second."

Dene laughed, "The police?" but nothing was funny. Aloura continued to watch Elias with guilty eyes as he thrashed around, his attempts to free himself were feeble. "The police Chief is a good friend of mine." He told them, before looking at his watch. "In fact, they should be here any minute now." Aloura's head snapped to Dene's smug look at this. The police chief's name was on the sheet of paper, she had counted for him to be the good cop. She swallowed and prayed the FBI would arrive soon; they were their only hope now.

Dene grabbed a gun from his waist band and turned it to Aloura's head. Elias cried out, "No. stop. I'll keep fighting." He hated the sound of what he had said, but it was much better than the sound of a life without Aloura.

Aloura's hands trembled, and awaited the gun shot, but footsteps filled the room instead. And all heads turned to the door.

Elias' eyes found Aloura in relief. She offered him a hopeful smile, and he struggled once more in the men's grip. They were more muscular than Elias, and had been trained in holding hostages, Elias knew he stood no chance against them, especially now more officers had found their way to them.

Elias' and Blayde's bodies were pushed to their knees, and guns placed at the temple of their heads. Aloura's eyes widened at the sight, she turned to Dene and cried, "Please, just shoot me and let them go."

"Aloura stop talking" Elias snapped, he didn't mean to raise his voice at her, but he couldn't let her offer her life for his freedom. Aloura looked at him, and back at Dene. Elias' eyes remained transfixed to Aloura as Blayde turned and grabbed the barrel of the gun held at his head. Gun shots hit the ground.

Elias struggled again before turning to Blayde, who had now freed himself in the commotion, he watched as Blayde wrestled his hands for the gun. Shots rang through the room, and various sounds of panic bounced off the walls. Blayde positioned the gun at Dene's direction, before pulling the trigger once.

Except three shots filled the room.

Aloura heard Elias' scream before she felt the bullets.

It wasn't until she'd placed her hands on her stomach and lifted them to her eyes did she realise she had been shot. Her knees buckled beneath her, and her ears rang. Aloura felt Elias' hands holding her falling body as he guided them onto the floor. "Aloura" he cried to her, his hands shaking above the wound before pressing down on it. He turned to the people in the room. "Call a fucking ambulance." He called out to no one in particular. "Call a fucking ambulance." His words barely audible through his sobs.

Aloura looked at him and frowned, her ears were ringing, and her world had begun to spin. She placed her hands over Elias' and felt the blood that spilled from her. The thought of it left her nauseous. At least she could see two of Elias.

Elias watched Aloura as she looked around the room with distant eyes, he called for her, but Aloura could barely make out his words. She forced a blink to clear her eyes. Why was she crying? She lifted her bloodied her hand once again and pressed them onto the wound which was covered by Elias' larger ones. She swallowed and looked down once again at her bloodied hands. She could feel herself scream, but not hear it. She'd almost thought her screams had deafened her, but Elias moved one hand up to her face and shook her gently. Snapping her back from wherever her body had floated too.

Elias felt helpless as he watched Aloura cry out in pain, her eyes now tightly shut. "It hurts so bad Eli" she cried, wincing as he applied more pressure. Her words only made Elias sob harder.

"I know baby, I know. I'm sorry." he told her. But it wasn't his fault, Aloura didn't regret it, and she would do it again if it came down to it. He was worth dying for. "The ambulance is on their way baby." He reminded her, unsure if he only kept saying it to console himself or Aloura. He pressed the wound again and buried his face in her hair like he did in the rooftop.

Elias watched her twitching chest, heaving as she struggled for a breath. Aloura groaned and turned to the boy covered in her blood. "Are you going to call Kalian now?" she gasped at him, as she forced her eyes open. Elias lifted Aloura's frail body and pulled her into his lap, cradling her.

Elias didn't hear the FBI entering the room, as his eyes remained on Aloura,, his hands pressed against her wound. "Yes baby, stay with me so we can call him together okay?" He didn't try hiding the tears in his eyes as she watched him with a small smile. "He asked to talk to you."

Tears ran down Aloura's neck, she knew she'd never have the chance now. Aloura shook her head meekly. "No. no, you gonna be free when I'm gone."

Elias shook his head; she was going to make it alive. He'd sell his soul for Aloura to make it out of tonight. "Blayde shot him baby, he's gone. I'm free so stay with me so we can be free together." Aloura smiled through the agonising pain, she liked the sound of that. Free together. But she did not let herself indulge in the idea, she wasn't going to make it alive, she could feel it. Elias placed pressure on her stomach, and she cried out in pain. He flinched at the sound.

"He shot him?" her eyes closed for a moment, but a small smile tugged at her lips.

Elias nodded; it was getting harder to see Aloura through his tears. "The Ambulance is on its way baby, please hold on." He reminded her pressing the wound again and burying his face in her hair, inhaling her scent. He was confident that when they'd gotten here, they'd patch her up like new. They'd go home together after that, and get Kalian, maybe even apply to a couple of colleges together. But Aloura, and everyone else in the room could see the ending of this story.

"Can you hold my hand?" her voice broke as she cried. She was suddenly scared, she wasn't ready to die. Elias looked up at a tearful Blayde, who took his place by Aloura's wound as Elias grasped Aloura's hands. She intertwined their fingers, and Elias lifted it to his lips and kissed her bloodied knuckles. Aloura closed her eyes and Elias shook her gently, his eyes fell to her gushing wound, and the blood that pooled beneath her, his heart sinking, and sobs racked his body at the realisation.

"Can I see your pretty eyes Aloura?"

Aloura forced her eyes open, "Did you win?" Elias smiled through his sobs. He turned to Blayde, and they shared a sad laugh.

"Of course I won, you're my lucky charm remember?"

Aloura whimpered and nodded, she'd never forget that. "You won't need me anymore now you're free" she joked, although she meant it.

"I'll always need you." His voice broke, and Aloura's eyes fluttered shut.

'Then you'll always have me." Elias' shoulders shook as he held her almost limp frame, wishing he was on the rooftop with Aloura's body pressed onto his instead, or somewhere sharing their food even though they both had their own.

He didn't reply to her, instead turned to the people gathered around him. "Where is the fucking Ambulance?" he yelled, they murmured an 'on its way' but Elias didn't wait for a reply. He'd already turned to cradle the girl in his arms. She'd already lost so much blood.

"Eli?" Aloura called, her eyes now remained shut, and blood specked her words. He hummed in response, not trusting his voice to speak. Elias pressed his face into the crook of her neck as Aloura gathered enough breath to speak.

"Can you stay with me until it stops hurting?" Elias nodded, he'd never dream of leaving her.

"You're going to be okay baby. The ambulance will come and they're gonna patch you as good as new" Aloura shook her head as tears spilled from her eyes, pooling with her blood beneath her. "They will baby they will." He told her, his voice desperate.

Aloura shook her head again, and her eyes fluttered shut. "I'm going to close my eyes now" she told him, it was now Elias' turn to frantically shake his head.

"No, Aloura." he turned to the people and cried "Please. The ambulance'" before turning back to Aloura who's eyes now shut. He shook her gently, and she pried them open, before shutting them again "Aloura." He cried.

"It doesn't hurt anymore Eli, please don't cry." Elias only sobbed harder.

"Please you're going to be okay. Okay?" he turned to her wound to make sure Blayde was holding it correctly. Aloura lips lifted into a small smile as her eyes remained shut.

"I'm going to wait for you on the brightest star. Okay?" Elias shook his head again and cried, but Aloura's hand that remained intertwined with Elias' grew limp as soon as the words left her lips.

 Elias body shook as he readjusted Aloura into his arms, his hand still entangled with hers. "Aloura" he called out, shaking her. "Aloura?" She gave him no reply, he turned to Blayde who watched the scene beside him with broken eyes.

He shook his head as tears fell from his eyes, a sob slipping from his lips "she's gone man" he told Elias who stared at him with wide eyes.

Elias shook his head frantically and frowned at Blayde, "What're you doing?" he cried out, shifting her limp body on his lap, she had to be comfortable. He nudged Blayde who let him. "Press on the wound man. What're you doing. Press on the wound."

Blayde only sobbed in response. Elias watched Aloura's still chest with wide eyes and quivering lips. His eyes searching for any sign of a flicker of life. He swallowed when he found none and collapsed onto her chest. "Wake up baby" he cried into her, "please wake up."

"We haven't even finished reading our book yet."

Chapter Thirty Five

Four years later

Elias fisted the soil that covered his beloved and half his heart, his eyes tracing the engraved words on the slab of stone. Aloura Olea West.

 He swallowed and looked away; her name was almost unbearable; a constant reminder that she was merely a memory now. "I'm sorry I don't come here often." He told her gently, blinking away the tears that filled his eyes. "For the longest time I couldn't even bare to hear your name."

"It reminded that I'd have to live with your memory for longer than I had you."

"I still wake up with things to tell you." He fisted the soil again and dropped it, not caring that it now filled his nails.

He smiles softly at the flowers Annie had probably placed earlier that day. "I didn't even know how to talk about you without feeling like I'd lost you all over again." He laughed like it was funny. "And I was scared to change because" he swallowed his tears, "I was scared to be someone you don't know." He wiped his tears with his sleeve and sniffled. "Because what if you don't love that version of me?"

 "Sorry, I didn't mean to come here and depress you." He laughed, "I actually have something useful to say." He laughed again and lifted his arm to his head. "Aloura" He looked at the sky and back at the headstone, before grabbing his mortarboard cap and placing it on the soil. "Ask me if I went to college baby."

He paused, as if waiting for Aloura to ask. And after a moment he smiled and nodded. "Yeah, I went to college."

♡ ♡ ♡

"It's your graduation and you want to have a picnic here?" Kalian laughed; Elias laughed too because Kalian would never understand how this rooftop had saved him. "What's with your obsession with this place anyway?"

Elias looked at his little brother and smiled gently, "Its where Aloura is"

"The chick waiting for you in the stars?" Kalian laughed again, but Elias didn't take offence. He'd understand one day.

At the mention of the stars, Elias eyes look up to find the new star positioned next to the one Aloura had pointed out as her mother. He grins and the star glistens back.

"Yep" Elias smiles at her memory, "that's my girl."

The End

Aloura's letter

Elias, my love.

I told you breaking a pinkie promise would cost you your pinkie, I guess it cost me my life instead. But I would do it again and again a thousand times if you got to live the life you deserved. And I'm praying that when you read this letter, it'll be the start of that life.

I got to live the life I dreamed about the day I laid my eyes on you. And I think it's time I told you that since you've entered my life, I no longer needed to hang off the rooftop to feel alive, because you did that for me.

Thank you for being my high Elias, and thank you for making a home in my heart.

We never got to say this, but I love you Elias Kader, and I'll keep loving you even after my last breath.

 Look for me in the stars will you?

Lots of love, Aloura.

Authors note:

If you've made it this far I fucking love you.

This is my first official book so please be kind, but constructive criticism is both welcomed and encouraged on both my social media pages and in my dm's. Also I apologise to any of my teachers, friends, siblings and my mum and dad who've just had to read my smut lmao. Ily <3

Also, I have so many more books I'm writing, including the 'I see colour' mentioned in this book. So, if you'd like to be kept updated on my future work follow me on my social medias, or don't and just check periodically. Whatever you want.

Instagram: x.ebzz
Tok-tok: urarabauthor

Bye for now, I love you :)

Printed in Great Britain
by Amazon